MAR 0 2 2017

# GRAFFITI MOON

CATH CROWLEY

GRAFFITI
MOON

EMBER

Text copyright © 2010, 2012 by Cath Crowley
Cover photograph copyright © 2012 by Jamaica Sandoval
Cover illustrations copyright © 2012 by Shutterstock

All rights reserved. Published in the United States by Ember, an imprint of Random House Children's Books, a division of Random House, Inc., New York. Originally published in paperback in Australia by Pan Macmillan Australia Pty Limited, Sydney, in 2010, and subsequently published in slightly different form in hardcover in the United States by Alfred A. Knopf, an imprint of Random House Children's Books, New York, in 2012.

Ember and the E colophon are registered trademarks of Random House, Inc.

Visit us on the Web! randomhouse.com/teens

Educators and librarians, for a variety of teaching tools, visit us at
RHTeachersLibrarians.com

The Library of Congress has cataloged the hardcover edition of this work as follows:
Crowley, Cath.
Graffiti moon / Cath Crowley. — 1st American ed.
p. cm.
Summary: Told in alternating voices, an all-night adventure featuring Lucy, who is determined to find an elusive graffiti artist named Shadow, and Ed, the last person Lucy wants to spend time with, except for the fact that he may know how to find Shadow.
ISBN 978-0-375-86953-2 (trade) — ISBN 978-0-375-96953-9 (lib. bdg.) —
ISBN 978-0-375-98365-8 (ebook)
[1. Artists—Fiction. 2. Graffiti—Fiction. 3. Interpersonal relations—Fiction. 4. Australia—Fiction.]
I. Title.
PZ7.C88682Gr 2012
[Fic]—dc22
2011003925

ISBN 978-0-375-87195-5 (pbk.)

RL: 6.0

Printed in the United States of America

10 9 8 7 6 5 4 3

First Ember Edition 2012

Random House Children's Books supports the First Amendment and celebrates the right to read.

TO TERESA AND EVERYONE IN THE ROOM.
AND TO ESTHER, WHO READ IT FIRST.

# LUCY

I pedal fast. Down Rose Drive, where houses swim in pools of orange streetlight. Where people sit on verandas, hoping to catch a breeze. Let me make it in time. Please let me make it in time.

*Just arrived at the studio. Your graffiti guys Shadow and Poet are here,* Al texted, and I took off across the night. Took off under a sky bleeding out and turning black. Left Dad sitting outside his shed yelling, "I thought you weren't meeting Jazz till later. Where's the fire, Lucy Dervish?"

In me. Under my skin.

Let me make it in time. Let me meet Shadow. Poet too but mainly Shadow. The guy who paints in the dark. Paints birds trapped on brick walls and people lost in ghost forests. Paints guys with grass growing from their hearts and girls with buzzing lawn mowers. An artist who paints things like that is someone I could fall for. Really fall for.

I'm so close to meeting him, and I want it so bad. Mum

says when wanting collides with getting, that's the moment of truth. I want to collide. I want to run right into Shadow and let the force spill our thoughts so we can pick each other up and pass each other back like piles of shiny stones.

At the top of Singer Street I see the city, neon blue and rising. There's lightning deep in the sky, working its way through the heat to the surface. There's laughter somewhere far away. There's one of Shadow's pieces, a painting on a crumbling wall of a heart cracked by earthquake with the words *Beyond the Richter scale* written underneath. It's not a heart like you see on a Valentine's Day card. It's the heart how it really is: fine veins and atriums and arteries. A fist-size forest in our chest.

I take my hands off the brakes and let go. The trees and the fences mess together and the concrete could be the sky and the sky could be the concrete and the factories spread out before me like a light-scattered dream.

I turn a corner and fly down Al's street. Toward his studio, toward him sitting on the steps, little moths above him, playing in the light. Toward a shadow in the distance. A shadow of Shadow. There's collision up ahead.

I spin the last stretch and slide to a stop. "I'm here. I made it. Do I look okay? How do I look?"

Al drains his coffee and puts the cup on the step beside him. "Like a girl who missed them by about five minutes."

# ED

It's a sweating hot night for October. More people are out than usual, so I spray the sky fast. Eyes ahead and behind. Looking for cops. Looking for anyone I don't want to be here. Paint sails and the things that kick in my head scream from can to brick. See this, see this, see this. See me emptied onto a wall.

First thing I ever painted was a girl. Second thing I ever painted was a doorway on a brick wall. Went on to paint huge doorways. Moved on to skies. Open skies painted above painted doorways and painted birds skimming across bricks trying to fly away. Little bird, what are you thinking? You come from a can.

Tonight I'm doing this bird that's been in my head all day. He's a little yellow guy lying on sweet green grass. Belly to clouds, legs facing the same direction. He could be sleeping. He could be dead. The yellow's right. The green too. The sky's all wrong. I need the sort of blue that rips your inside out. You don't see blue like that round here.

Bert was always trying to find it for me. Every week or so at the paint store he'd show me a blue he'd special-ordered. "Close, boss," I'd say. "But not close enough."

He still hadn't found it when he died two months ago. He got all the other colors I wanted. The green this bird's lying on is a shade he found over two years back, after I quit school and went to work for him. I made it to the end of June in year ten, and then I couldn't make it any longer.

"You had a good first day," Bert told me when he handed the green over. "Real good."

"This is very fucking nice," I said, spraying some on a card and taking it as a sign that leaving school was the right thing to do. That Mum was wrong about wanting me to stay on.

"It is very fucking nice." Bert looked over his shoulder. "But don't say 'fuck' when my wife Valerie's around." Bert always swore like a kid scared of getting caught. I laughed about it till Val heard me swearing. Bert had the last chuckle that day.

"What's so funny?" a voice behind me asks.

"Shit, Leo." A line of blue goes into the grass on the wall. "Don't sneak up."

"I've been calling your name since the top of the hill. And the council made this place legal, remember?" He finishes the last bit of his sausage roll. "I like the rush of working where we might get caught."

"I like the rush of painting," I tell him.

He watches me for a bit. "So I called your mobile earlier. It's disconnected."

4

"Uh-huh. Didn't pay the bill." I hand him the can. "I'm hungry. Write the words."

Leo looks at my picture of a wide sky hanging over that yellow bird. He points at the kid on the wall. "Nice touch."

While he thinks a bit longer, I look around. The old guy who works at the glass studio across the road is on the steps, texting and staring at us. At least I know he's not calling the cops.

Leo always makes his writing suit the piece. Sometimes he uses fonts he finds online. Sometimes he makes up his own and names them. Tonight he smokes the word *Peace* across the clouds, letters drifting and curling. It's funny how two guys can look at the same thing and see it differently. I don't see peace when I look at that bird. I see my future. I hope it's only sleeping.

His hand moves across the wall, signing our names. He always writes them the same way. His, then mine, in a font he calls Phantasm.

*Poet.*

*Shadow.*

We leave the old guy on the steps with his coffee and head up Vine Street. It's a fifteen-minute walk to my place if you take the main roads, but Leo and me never do. We take the side streets and alleys.

I live on the other side of the train yard, so we jump the fence and cut through, looking out for people working as we walk. I like seeing their thoughts hit the carriages. Makes the city as much ours as someone else's.

"So I saw Beth today," Leo says. "She asked me how you were doing." He throws stones at the dead trains. "It sounded like she wants you back."

I stop and take out a can and spray a greeting-card heart with a gun pointed at it. "We've been over almost three months." Since August first, not that I'm counting.

"You mind if I ask her out, then?"

"You mind if I spray a piece on the side of your gran's house?"

He chuckles. "Yeah, right. You're over."

"I like her, just not anything more than that. She used to do this thing where she'd lean over and kiss me and then take a break to whisper hilarious stuff in my ear and then kiss me again. I'd be screaming, What's wrong with you? Fall in love with her, you dick."

"She didn't think that was weird?"

"Inside. I was screaming on the inside. Anyway, I never fell in love with her so I guess the part of the brain that controls love doesn't respond to being called a dick."

"For your sake, I'm hoping no part of your brain responds to being called a dick."

"Fair point." I wish I hadn't thought about Beth doing that thing because now I can feel her at my ear, warm breath and sweet tickling and her voice sounding like that blue I've been searching for.

"Were you in love with Emma?" I ask.

"I was hard-core obsessed," he says without thinking about it. "Not in love."

6

"What's the difference?"

He's about to throw a stone at a yard light but stops. "Prison," he says, and puts the stone in his pocket.

Emma dumped him at the end of year eleven. I wasn't at school then so the first I heard of it was when he came into the shop yelling that he needed me to paint a wall on the side of Emma's house.

"She doesn't know I'm Poet," he said. "If she knows she'll take me back."

Emma lived in the good part of town in a three-story terrace. We weren't painting anything on that and getting away with it. The night'd end badly and I knew it but there was no talking Leo down so I told him I'd get the paint and meet him there at ten.

Bert saw my backpack full of cans as I was leaving. He'd known I was Shadow since my first week working for him. His rule was that I painted on things that didn't belong to anyone, so most of the time that's what I did. "Be careful," he said.

"'No guts, no glory,' isn't that what you're always saying?" I asked.

His shaggy old face stared me down. "Don't go confusing stupidity with guts."

He had a point but I sprayed what Leo wanted anyway: a guy with the word *love* cut out of his chest and a girl next to him holding some scissors. Emma came out and saw it and he got on his knees in front of that wall, a love-cut guy begging her to take him back.

She pulled out her mobile phone and called the cops. Leo wouldn't leave and I wouldn't leave without him and about ten minutes later we were in the back of a police van headed for fingerprinting. "It's lucky we didn't sign our names, hey?" Leo asked. "We'd be in trouble if she'd told them we were Poet and Shadow."

"Uh-huh," I said while the drunk guy opposite yelled he'd fucking kill everyone when the cuffs came off. "Good thing you were thinking tonight or we'd really be in trouble."

We gave our statements and Leo told the cops everything, about being dumped, about wanting Emma back. They must have thought she was pretty cold because they called my mum and Leo's gran and let us off with a warning and on the understanding that we'd clean up the mess we'd made. I never heard Leo's gran yell so much as when she was dragging him toward the car. He's been mowing lawns on Saturdays for her friends ever since.

Mum was quiet when they brought me out of the holding cell. She still had her supermarket uniform on, her badge telling everyone her name was Maddie: she hoped they had a nice day. I always hated that badge because she looked so tired when she was wearing it.

"How mad are you?" I asked after we got in the car.

She started the engine and her Smashing Pumpkins CD screamed out of the player.

"Question answered."

After driving awhile, she turned down the music. "Is this what you and Leo get up to, now that I'm back at school and working nights?"

If she'd been looking right at me and not at the road I would have told her the truth. "It was this one time. Emma dumped Leo and he wanted her back."

"So, of course, he vandalized her house. I love Leo like a son but he's got to grow up sometime. So do you."

"I'm grown up. I'm sixteen. I've got a job."

"I had a baby *and* a job at sixteen. I wasn't grown up."

She parked in front of our flat block, which is shoved into the end of Pitt Street. We stared at the four floors of orange brick and the balconies growing washing-line gardens. "Maybe I should quit nursing school and go back to working days until you're eighteen."

It'd taken me a year to talk her into applying for nursing school. She got in and I started paying half the rent so she could cut her shifts and work nights. "If you quit, then you'll always be here," I told her.

"And where will you be, Ed?"

I didn't answer.

"That's what I'm worried about."

She didn't quit but I knew she would if I got caught again so for a week I didn't do any walls. But they were all I thought about and by Friday I was painting again. I worked inside the old caravan near the skate park so no one would see.

I told Leo what she'd said about us growing up while we were sweating and cleaning off paint. Emma walked past us with her friends. "No offense to your mum, but fuck growing up," he said, staring at her till she disappeared.

• • •

Leo and I jump the train yard fence and cut down the last alley that leads to Pitt Street. People's windows are open in our flat block, letting out heat and the sound of music and TVs. Mum and me have been here since I was eight. She wanted me to have my own room and this was all we could afford.

Before Pitt Street we were in a one-bedroom place. Gran had moved into a home after Granddad died so we had to go out on our own. The flat had orange carpet and floral wall-paper but Mum looked at it and said, "It's ugly but it's bigger than the others. And ugly I can do something about."

We didn't have the money for bookshelves so Mum used two old ladders she'd found in the street. She set them up at either end of the lounge room and filled them with stuff like her collection of snow globes and vinyl albums and the Pez collection Grandma had left me. I got the bedroom, and to make herself a place to sleep, Mum tied string between the ladders and ran a silk curtain across. Around the kitchen win-dow she strung fairy lights and together we put stick-on stars all over my ceiling. When the main lights were off, I couldn't see the stains on the carpet and the walls.

The first poem Leo wrote was about night at our place. Our year-four teacher didn't put it on the wall because he wouldn't change it like she wanted. Mum framed his words and hung them in the lounge room without him changing a thing.

*The stars are inside. It's very fucking beautiful.*

When we moved into Pitt Street it was ugly like the last

place but Mum made it okay. She had enough money for real bookshelves and we didn't need the silk across the lounge anymore. She bought a lamp on a long base with a red shade because I liked it. My room had a spare bed in it for Leo.

"What do you think?" she asked the day we moved in.

"Feels like home," I said. It didn't feel so small or gray back then.

I flick on the light and Leo looks in the fridge for food. Comes up empty. I flick the air-con switch. Nothing happens. I smack it. Leo smacks it. He almost knocks it off the wall but it still doesn't give any air. "We're not meant to get hot days like this in October," I say, standing in front of the open freezer.

"Don't start. Gran's been complaining about Melbourne weather all day. I told her, 'You live in Australia, that's what you get.'"

"What'd she say?"

"She made me clean out the shed."

"That's what I thought." Leo's one of the toughest guys around, but his gran's tougher.

"Is your mum at work?" he asks.

"It's her night off. She's out at some big deal hocus-pocus night at the casino. Getting her fortune read. It's an all-night thing because 'magic' happens in the early hours."

He chuckles.

"Not that sort of magic."

I shut the freezer and watch him lean against the bench;

his legs almost reach the other side of the kitchen. This place feels even smaller than it did when we moved in, but it isn't the size that bothers me. It's the gray that's worked its way into the walls over the years. It's the stains on the carpet from some other life that came and left before ours. After I'd been working at the store for a month, Bert said he'd give me a good deal on paint. Mum would have used it if I'd told her but I knew it'd be a waste of time. Some places take burning down and rebuilding to make them shiny.

"So, I finished year twelve today," Leo says. "How about we go out, have some food at Feast, meet some girls?"

"I got exactly fifteen dollars left in the world."

He looks past me at the calendar and the circle around rent day. "No luck getting another job?"

"Negative luck. People don't even return my calls."

"I'm helping Jake this morning if you're interested. We can get five hundred bucks each for two hours' work starting at three a.m. All we have to do is pick up the van, load it, drive it away."

"Are you stupid?" I ask.

"That's what it says on my report cards."

"Don't even joke about this. Your brother gets caught every single time." Right back to when he was fifteen and he talked some guy at a car dealership into letting him take a Jag for a test-drive. He's even taller than Leo, so the guy believed his fake license. Plus, Jake's got a way of talking that makes people believe.

Instead of driving the Jag somewhere no one knew him,

he rolled around the block near his house, music vibrating through the windows. His gran pulled him out by the ear in front of everyone on the street.

Leo reaches over and hits the air-con again. "I owe some money."

He looks worried, which gets me worried because a team of footballers coming at him in a dark alley doesn't bother him too much. That leaves one person. "Tell me you don't owe money to Malcolm Dove."

He looks out the window.

"Shit, Leo. Shit. The guy's crazy."

"Define crazy."

"Eating a cockroach for a dare," I say.

Leo shrugs. "Okay, so he's crazy. All the more reason to give him his money."

I fish in the back of the cupboard for some chips and think about the seriousness of the situation. Malcolm's about the same age as Jake but they're not friends. Malcolm doesn't have friends. He has a group of thugs who hang around, doing him favors.

"Why'd you need five hundred dollars that bad?" I ask. "You mow lawns every Saturday."

"Yeah, well, old ladies mostly pay in food. And my gran needed some things." He taps on the counter. "Malcolm's coming for me tonight. I'm two months late with the payment."

For Leo's sake I try not to look worried.

"Look. All I need to do is dodge him till three o'clock and I'll have the money."

"You can't ask Jake for an advance?"

"I don't want him knowing I owe Malcolm."

"Has he been round to your house?" I ask.

"No. But I'm guessing he'll pay Gran a visit if he doesn't get what he's owed tonight. Dylan said he'd help. One job and we all start the month even. We've got at least a first offense before the cops even think about putting us in jail."

"That's one bright future up ahead." I think about Mum adding bleak numbers in the night, about her seeing psychics and looking for happy endings.

"My son needs a job," the new owner of the paint store said when he sacked me six weeks ago. "It's nothing personal." Funny. Our landlord is taking it real personal.

Dylan calls Leo and while they're talking I flick through Bert's little sketchbook. Valerie gave it to me at the funeral. "You're his wife, it belongs to you," I told her. She held it out in the space between us till I took it.

During our lunch breaks at the shop Bert'd sit there talking and drawing these pictures. Each one was on a different page, drawn almost the same as the one before. His old hands moved while he talked and by the end of lunch he'd always finished a new series. I'd flick the pages and the thing he'd drawn moved like a cartoon.

I look at one he drew of me while I wait for Leo. I watch myself eat sandwiches and talk to Bert while the clouds roll over my head, backward and forward.

Leo hangs up and writes something down. I never could get my handwriting to look like his. Sundays after football in year five he'd take my hand and move it across the page for me till I got so mad I'd snap the pencil. Leo'd laugh and pull out another pencil. "My handwriting should be better than yours," I'd tell him. "You can't even draw." He'd shrug. You get what you get.

"I told Dylan we'd meet him at the school on the way to Feast. We'll get some food and stick together till it's time," he says. "So?"

So I want to go back to when I had enough money to pay the rent without stealing. I want to go back to when Bert was alive and telling me to do my own thinking. I want to fast-forward to when Mum's a nurse and earning a full wage. "I'm in," I say, and close the book on the picture of me sitting with Bert, eating lunch and talking under those rolling clouds.

The school's only a few streets away from my place, in the opposite direction to the train yard. I hate that it's so close because there's no way to avoid the kids in uniforms.

I sketched a picture of it one day while I was sitting with Bert. Buildings surrounded by wire and a little guy caught in the barbs. Bert looked at it over my shoulder. "Is he trying to get in or get out?" he asked. I wasn't exactly sure.

Dylan's waiting for us, sitting in front of a wall that says *Dylan loves Daisy* in big red letters. Leo looks at it for a while. "We're robbing this place later and you're signing your name on the wall? Did you remember to leave the art-wing window open this afternoon?"

"Of course I did."

"Robbing the art wing? That's mean," I say.

"It's where they keep the computers. What do you care anyway? They kicked you out," Dylan says.

"Shut up," Leo tells him. "Ed left because he wanted to leave."

And they start arguing about whether graffiti's admissible evidence in court. Dylan tells him there's nothing to connect him, not even paint on his hands. "I wore rubber gloves." He points at the pink pair next to him on the seat. "That paint is toxic."

"How about we don't make ourselves memorable in any way tonight," Leo says. I watch him sweating and I plan a piece I could paint, a guy with his back to the wall, crowded by dollar signs that are about to kick the life out of him. The cops won't care why Leo, Dylan, and I need the money. All they'll care about is that we're filling the van with things that aren't ours.

While they're yelling I spray every corner of the wall so there's nothing to say I was ever here, and as I'm doing it a siren goes off not far away. "I got a bad feeling," I tell them, but my voice gets lost in the mix of the city.

# POET

Assignment One
Poetry 101
Student: Leopold Green

**Where I lived before**

I used to live with my parents
In a house that smelled like cigarettes
And tasted like beer if you touched anything
The kitchen table was a bitter ocean
That came off on my fingers

There were three doors between the fighting and me
And at night I closed them all
I'd lie in bed and block the sounds

By imagining
I was floating

Light-years of quiet
Interrupted by breathing
And nothing else

I'd drift through space
And fall through dreams
Into dark skies

Some nights
My brother Jake and I would crawl out the window
And cut across the park
Swing on the monkey bars for a while
On the way to Gran's house

She'd be waiting
Dressing gown and slippers on
Searching for our shadows

She'd read us
Poetry and fairy tales
Where swords took care of dragons
And Jake never said it was a load of shit
Like I thought he would

And then one night
Gran stopped reading before the happy ending
She asked, "Leopold, Jake. You want to live
In my spare room?"

Her voice
Sounded like space and dark skies
But that night all my dreams
Had floors

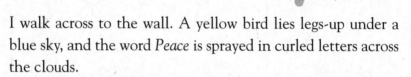

# LUCY

I walk across to the wall. A yellow bird lies legs-up under a blue sky, and the word *Peace* is sprayed in curled letters across the clouds.

"I guess it's too late to give peace a chance," Al says. "Looks like it's dead."

"Nope," I say. "It's only sleeping."

Most times when I look at Shadow and Poet's work I see something different from what the words are telling me. I like that about art, that what you see is sometimes more about who you are than what's on the wall. I look at this painting and think about how everyone has some secret inside, something sleeping like that yellow bird.

I look and get a feeling, a sort of zing. That zing has nothing to do with sex like my best friend, Jazz, says. Okay, in the interest of honesty, maybe it's got a little to do with sex, but mainly it's got to do with knowing that there's a guy out there who's not like all the other guys out there.

"I need more details," I say, my eyes still on the wall.

"It's like I told you. Shadow does the painting. Poet writes the words."

"Did you get a better look this time?"

"Same look I had before. They're young and scruffy," Al says. "About your age."

"Cute?"

"I'm a sixty-year-old man. I really couldn't say."

"Which direction did they go?"

"My street hits a dead end, Lucy. They went in the only direction they could."

I sit next to him and concentrate really hard.

"What are you doing?" he asks.

"Trying to bend the laws of time so I can get here five minutes earlier."

He nods, and we watch the dirty silk of the factory smoke float across the sky. "Any luck?" he asks after a while.

"Nope."

"You'll see him. It's just a matter of time. Since this place became legal, Shadow's been working here a bit." He looks at his watch. "So you finished year twelve today. Are you and Jazz hitting the town?"

"We're meeting at Feast Café around nine-thirty."

"Late start."

"Jazz wants a late-night, all-night adventure."

"Is there time to help me with a piece before you go?" he asks, and I nod and follow him inside.

I'm addicted to this place. To the heat coming off the

furnace. To my muscles aching as I help Al blow glass. I ache with the weight of the piece on the end of the pipe. Ache with the thought that in a place as ugly as this, a place of rust and sweat and steel, something shining like love can appear.

I've got Mrs. J., my art teacher, to thank for introducing me to Al. In year ten she took us on an excursion to his studio, and we stood behind a wire safety fence and watched him blow glass. The heat from the furnaces was burning me up but it felt like it was happening from the inside out. I'd never wanted to do something so bad.

Al offered a free six-week glassblowing course to one of Mrs. J.'s students, and she gave it to me. I was meant to arrive at seven in the morning on my first day, but I was so excited I turned up at six-thirty. Al was already there, humming along to Johnny Cash and melting cheese on toast with a blowtorch.

"Good," he said, switching off the torch. "You're in time for breakfast."

We sat on the steps and ate buckled cheese that tasted better than anything I'd ever had. "We call this place a hot shop, because the furnaces in there are heated to over two thousand degrees Fahrenheit," Al said. "You ever been burned by something that hot?"

"Nope," I told him.

"Let's keep it that way. You do what I tell you, wear what I tell you, and learn what I tell you."

I nodded.

"Are you quiet because you're nervous?" he asked.

"I'm quiet because I'm excited." I told him about how I

felt, watching him make glass. It was like he was hatching a world from a ball of honey.

"The first time I watched a glassblower I couldn't think of anything to say," he said, standing up. "I was nothing inside but light and color."

After the course was done Al said he'd keep being my teacher. I worked off half my costs by cleaning his studio every week. Mum and Dad paid the other half. I've been cleaning and taking lessons here ever since. Yesterday, thanks to Al, I finished my year-twelve art folio.

"Concentrate," he says tonight, and uses wet newspaper to turn and shape the shiny mass. He nods, and I blow into the mouthpiece and cover the opening with my thumb to trap the air; the vase inflates with my breath. When he nods I put the piece into the glory hole to maintain the temperature. "You have to work quickly with glass," Al told me on my first day. "We heat it in the glory hole or we blowtorch it to maintain the temperature. Too cool and it cracks. Too hot and it loses its shape. But know the properties and you can make it almost anything you want." That day he breathed a sun into existence.

I pull the piece out of the furnace and rest it on the bench, spinning the pipe slowly. Al uses the newspaper to turn and shape some more. The paper heats and burns, flecking the air with stars.

When we're done, his old hands move smooth as water as he cracks the glass off the end without breaking it. After we've put it in the annealer to cool, he says, "I think you're ready for a promotion. I thought you could keep working here while you're at college and I'd pay you in cash instead of in classes. No cleaning. Strictly glasswork."

"You're serious? I'd be your assistant?"

"You'd work with Jack and Liz. You interested?"

Al's one of the top glass artists in the city. I nod so much there's a nodding festival going on. "Good," he says. "Good."

We sit outside for a bit longer, me hoping that Shadow will make a return appearance. I get this heavy feeling when I daydream about him. I'm not awake and I'm not asleep. I'm in a soft blue corridor that runs between the two.

"How are things at home?" Al asks.

"Okay. Better. Dad's still living in the shed, but he comes into the house more and more, and not just to use the bathroom. I really think he'll be moving back in soon."

"That's great news."

"Yep. It was only ever meant to be a temporary move. And now they're not fighting anymore, so, you know." I look across at that sleeping bird. I imagine Shadow arcing his arm and spilling yellow across the gray. Spilling sunshine.

Mum's a part-time dental nurse and part-time novelist. Dad's a comedian-magician and a part-time taxi driver. For a couple of months before Dad moved into the shed, he and Mum had huge fights about stupid things. Then one day they just stopped. I came home from school and felt the quiet drifting along the street. When I walked into the yard, Dad was standing in front of the shed, sipping lemonade and cooking sausages and dehydrated potatoes over a little camp stove.

"What are you doing?" I asked.

"I'm moving into the shed for a while. Just till your mother finishes her novel and I get my next show written." He waved the barbecue tongs. "You want to have dinner at my place?"

"Your place is my place, Dad." I sat next to him while he cooked and I tried to figure things out. Sure they'd been fighting, but Dad and Mum had been together for thirty years. Dad was always going on about how romantic it was that they met in the university cafeteria. He asked for Mum's salt and she asked for his sugar. "Romance like that can't end in dehydrated potatoes," I said to Mum.

"Lucy, you're lucky if romance ends in something you can add water to and rehydrate," she answered.

This did not comfort me.

She ate dinner with us that night when she got home, which was even more confusing. They didn't fight. Mum told Dad the potatoes were delicious. "Stop looking at me like that," she said. "Your dad and I need space to write. I can't suck the saliva out of people's mouths for the rest of my life, and your dad can't drive a taxi."

I could understand that. Mum and Dad aren't exactly typical. She's got a picture of Orson Welles on her wall and wears a T-shirt to parent-teacher interviews that says IF YOU DON'T WANT A GENERATION OF ROBOTS, FUND THE ARTS. He can pull flowers out of his ears and juggle fire.

But they were always typical when it came to love and marriage. Dad's been out of the house for about six months now. He visits us quite a bit; he just lives in the shed. They seem happy, but if you ask me, the whole thing is weird.

"Who gets to say what's weird?" Mum asks when I bring up the subject.

"Me," I tell her. "I get to say."

She rolls her eyes.

I wheel my bike to the wall before I leave Al's. When I touch the painting some clear-blue sky comes off on my hands. I didn't notice before, but in the corner there's a confused kid staring at the bird. "There's a kid, did you see?" I call.

"I saw," he says.

I wave goodbye and push my bike up the hill. Jazz phones when I'm halfway to the top. "Daisy and I are already here. How far away are you?"

"I'm close. I took a detour because Shadow and Poet were at Al's."

"You saw them?"

"I missed them by five minutes but I have even more proof now that Shadow exists and that he's my age." I know exactly what she's going to say.

"Luce, his art's definitely cool, and I'm not saying don't make out with him if you meet him. But in the meantime, I could name at least one and a half guys who'd like to go out with you."

Okay, so I almost knew what she was going to say. "One and a *half*? Did some guy get caught in a bus door?"

"Simon Mattskey might be interested, but he's worried about the nose thing. I told him it was urban legend."

"I'm hanging up."

"Just remember, paintings proved that cavemen existed too. Shadow might not be the guy you've been waiting for."

I click my phone shut and take my time walking. Jazz thinks I haven't had enough action in the guy department. I've had action with other guys around here, and that's how I know that I don't want action with them again. The nose thing happened on June eleventh in year ten. It's not a date I'm likely to forget.

Jazz hadn't started at our school then, so she never heard the real story. By the time she arrived it had been mixed up, made bigger and half forgotten, and I wanted it to stay that way.

The guy was a sheddy, one of the kids who spent a lot of time leaning against the back sheds skipping classes. I'd seen him around before then but I never really noticed him till the start of year ten, when we were in the same art class.

It was an elective subject that year and I got the feeling he thought it'd be an easy option. Most times when I looked over he wasn't drawing. He was leaning back in his chair and staring at me. And every time he stared I felt like I'd touched my tongue to the tip of a battery. I was nothing but tingle. After a while the tingle turned to electricity, and when he asked me out my whole body amped to a level where technically I should have been dead. I was pretty sure we had nothing in common, but a girl doesn't think straight when she's that close to electrocution.

I liked that he had hair that was growing without a plan.

A smile that came out of nowhere and left the same way. That he was tall enough so I had to look up at him in my dream sequences. I really liked his T-shirts. When he asked me out he was wearing this one with a dog walking a man on a leash. And there was always this space around him. The sort of space you'd queue to get into.

Anyway. The night didn't go so well because I broke his nose, which was an accident that happened when I hit him in the face because he touched my arse.

Dad was still living in the house then, and before I left for the date, I told him all the things I hoped this guy and I would talk about. "Maybe *To Kill a Mockingbird*, the book we're studying. Maybe Rothko, the painter Mrs. J. showed us."

"Sounds like it'll be romantic," Dad said. "Your mum and I had a romantic first date. She was studying serious writing and I was studying comedy, so we went to a Woody Allen film that was somewhere in between. I don't remember the film, but I remember she smelled like sweet green tea."

I had that story in my head when I turned up for my date at Feast, the all-night café where the sheddies hang out. There wasn't any cool conversation, though. I asked him a couple of questions and he answered with a couple of sounds and we sat staring past each other at the walls until the food arrived. Then we sat staring at the food.

While we were walking to the movie I brought up *To Kill a Mockingbird* and he went to a level of quiet *beyond* the quiet we'd had before and grabbed my arse.

"Shit," he yelled as I elbowed him in the face. "Shit, I think you broke my nose."

"You shouldn't have grabbed my arse. You don't do that on a first date. Atticus Finch would never have done that."

"You're out with me and you have a boyfriend?" he yelled.

"No!"

"Then who the fuck is Atticus Finch?"

"He's in the book we're reading at school."

"You're talking to me about books? When I'm bleeding all over the road? Shit. *Shit*."

"Stop swearing at me." It was stupid to talk to him about books when it was my fault his shirt was covered in blood, but everything was going the opposite way to how I planned and I can't stand the sight of blood and I was so disappointed that he'd turned out to be an arse grabber that I ran and I didn't look back.

Mum took one glance at me when I got home and said, "Quick, over the laundry sink." She held my hair away from my face while I threw up so hard I almost flipped inside out. I didn't tell her what I'd done; I told her he wasn't who I thought he'd be. Mum stroked my hair and said, "Sometimes they aren't. Sometimes they make you vomit."

This did not comfort me.

But Shadow won't make me vomit. I feel very sure about that. He'll be a guy who talks about art, not an arse grabber. And like Dad says, love and romance are things worth waiting for.

At the top of the hill I start riding. The lights of the city reflect and bounce and I fly along my soft corridor thinking about Shadow. Somewhere in the glassy darkness, he's out there. Spraying color. Spraying birds and blue sky on the night.

I lock up my bike and walk into Feast. I don't come here all that often on account of it being the crime scene of my first date. Jazz and I mostly hang at the coffee shop on Kent Street. She works there every Saturday telling people's fortunes.

"I had my first experience at the age of five," she told me the day I met her. "I didn't know what *psychic* meant but I knew exactly where Mum had hidden the chocolate. And I knew exactly when to run so she didn't catch me eating it."

I stopped doubting her predictions after she told me I'd be allergic to guava juice, which was something I'd never tried. I drank a liter of it in the name of scientific research. Dad called me Big Face for weeks.

When I arrive she's sitting in the back booth, dressed for action and sucking on a lollipop. Mum leaves out horror dentist photos whenever Jazz stays over at my place. "Takes more than that to shock me, Mrs. Dervish," Jazz tells her. "I see into my future and my teeth are just fine." Mum rolls her eyes.

Her long, dark hair has little plaits and flowers here and there and she's wearing a pink dress and killer boots that she bought at a secondhand store on Delaney Street. The price tag said fifteen dollars but she beat the guy down to ten.

Before Jazz moved states and started at our school she went to Benton Girls' Grammar in Western Australia. The uniform there was a skirt that went below the knees, white socks that went above the knees, a white shirt, a tie, and a blazer. "You were pretty much strapped in," she said. "And there was no makeup, no jewelry, no *gum* allowed."

I had to see a school photo to believe it. Jazz wore the uniform, sure. But on the corner of the skirt she'd sewn a small blue flower. "Be un-uniform whenever possible, that was my rule," she said.

Next to her in the booth, Daisy's following the same rule. She's wearing a black singlet dress and green silk slippers. Her outfit matches her eyes. They're winter seas lashed with black that stand out even more because of her short blond hair. Her laugh makes me think of this piece Al made one day: dark violet glass curling out and upward. She's the sort of girl who gets stared at. She's the sort of girl who likes being stared at.

I check my reflection. I look like I slept in my faded jeans and Magic Dirt T-shirt. Maybe I did sleep in them, come to think of it. I pull up my hair and push a couple of paintbrushes through the bundle to keep it out of the way. Jazz gave me the tip about using them. My hair's too long for clips.

I slide into the booth.

"You're late." Jazz points her lollipop and gives me the serious look.

I steal a chip. "If the plan's to stay out all night, what's the hurry?"

"She's got a feeling," Daisy says. "The next guys to walk in here are the ones we're meant to hook up with."

"Have you seen the guys who live around here?" I ask.

"Lucy's right," Daisy says. "Some of them aren't pretty."

Daisy knows the crowd. She's a sheddy, so she comes here a lot. Jazz and I only started hanging out with her about a month back when we were put in an English group together. I always liked her; we just move in different crowds and go to different places.

Inviting her tonight was a spur-of-the-moment thing. She and Jazz and I were squashed behind a bush this afternoon, hiding from her boyfriend, Dylan, and his mates. They were slamming everyone with eggs to celebrate the end of year twelve.

"Romance is in serious need of some resuscitation," Daisy said while yolk slid down her face. She looked at Jazz and me, covered with egg. "I'm really sorry my boyfriend is such an idiot. I'm definitely breaking up with him. Tomorrow. If I do it before then I'll have no one to hang out with on the last night of year twelve."

"Hang out with us," Jazz said.

Another egg hit Daisy in the face. She didn't need much more convincing.

"Are you really breaking up with Dylan?" I ask while she's looking toward the toilet. "You've been together since the end of year ten."

"I really am. I don't know why I've stayed with him till now. It's too long to be explained by temporary insanity."

"Lucy's waiting for romance." Jazz says it like I'm the girl suffering from temporary insanity. "I'll settle for action. My parents are overseas at a law conference, so I've got one last night before year twelve is officially over. That's fifteen hours to make up for a year of solid study. I haven't had a date since midyear exams. Do you know what that does to a girl? Every entry in my year-twelve diary can't be: *Did homework, did more homework, watched TV, flossed, kissed my parents goodnight, secretly watched more TV.* Tomorrow I'm writing: *Stayed out all night. Kissed someone. End of year twelve.*"

Jazz wants to be an actress. She's applied for the bachelor of dramatic arts courses at the College of the Arts. She has to perform two monologues plus attend an interview. It's the monologues she's worried about, but I'm pretty sure she'll pass the audition. She's got a flair for drama.

"My teacher says I need some real emotion in my audition monologue. So if I don't kiss someone in the next twelve hours I'm going to regret it for the rest of my life."

"Kiss someone, then," I say. "Not anyone."

"Okay. I'll kiss someone cute. Like that," she says, pointing at the entrance.

"No way," Daisy and I say together.

"This is perfect." Jazz checks her reflection. "Leo Green's in my English class. I like the way he writes. I don't know the guy with him."

Daisy laughs. "It's Ed Skye. Lucy, you remember him?"

"Vaguely."

"He's hot," Jazz says. "Perfect for you."

Daisy stops laughing. "That leaves Dylan for me. I don't want Dylan."

"We'll find someone for you along the way," Jazz tells her. "Ready?"

"No," Daisy and I say.

"Good. We'll head over and let things unfold."

"I'd really like tonight to stay folded," I tell her.

"Not an option," Jazz says, handing Daisy and me a piece of gum each. I didn't seriously think it was.

Some things take forever. Waiting for a bus when it's raining. Getting waxed after winter. Lining up to get tickets for a band. Waiting for a coffee in the morning. The walk across to these guys isn't one of those things.

I blink and I'm staring past them through the window at the bridge. The lights on it are sending little warning messages: walk past the table, run, head to Al's, and wait on the steps for Shadow to come back.

"Hi," Jazz says, standing at the table.

Leo looks at her and grins. "Hi."

"Hi," Dylan says.

"Shut up," Daisy tells him, and makes the introductions. "Ed, this is Jazz Parker. Just a warning, she's psychic. So don't go thinking bad thoughts. You know Lucy. Leo, you know Jazz and Lucy. Jazz and Lucy, you know Dylan. He's the idiot who threw eggs at us today."

Ed looks at me like he wishes I'd disappear and if I had the choice I'd grant that wish; I'd turn into smoke and blow away. I want to sit on the other side of the table from him so he doesn't think I'm interested, but there's no room on the other side so I sit as far away from him as I can and try to have an out-of-body experience. This couldn't get more awkward if we all tried.

"How about we get some air?" Leo asks Jazz, and they walk outside. Daisy follows them and Dylan follows her. Okay, it could get more awkward if we all tried.

Don't think about Ed. Think about Shadow. Think about meeting him. Think about what you'll say, standing in front of him. Think about taking him into Al's studio and showing him shiny pink glazes that blaze in the light. Think about night slowly turning into day and Shadow not disappearing and you there, not disappearing with him.

I look over at Ed. He's staring out the window giving Leo the thumbs-down. I wait till he's looking at me, then I give him two fingers up. He gives me two fingers back. I give him the middle finger. He gives it back to me. I don't know any more signs, so I make up one. Three fingers. Take that, mister. He sticks up four. I call your four and raise you five. He skips straight to ten and does something with his thumb that disturbs me. I bounce my hands on my lap. Ed bounces his lap right back.

"Good." Jazz slides back into the booth. "You're talking."

"I can't believe you're still mad at me," Ed says.

"You grabbed my arse."

"You broke my nose."

"You broke his nose?" Jazz asks. "You grabbed her arse?"

"It was two years ago—"

"Two years, four months, and eight days," I tell him.

"—and I was fifteen, and I slipped and she broke my nose."

"Wait a minute. How do you slip onto someone's arse?" Jazz asks.

"I meant slipped up. I slipped up and she broke my nose."

"You're lucky that's all I broke," I say.

"You're lucky I didn't call the police."

Leo, Dylan, and Daisy slide into the booth. "Did you guys know that Lucy broke Ed's nose?" Jazz asks.

Ed closes his eyes and silently bangs his head on the wall.

"I took him to hospital," Leo says, grinning. "He had to sit for five hours in one of those gowns with his arse hanging out."

"His arse," Dylan says, hitting the table a few times.

Okay, if anyone says *arse* one more time I'm going to need some serious long-term therapy.

"I can't believe he grabbed your arse," Jazz says. "Your *arse*."

"Okay. I need a bathroom stop." I move out of the booth and put my hand on her back. "I have a feeling you need one too."

"Do I need one?" Daisy asks.

"Sure," I say. "Toilet stop for everyone." Leo grins and stands up. "Not you."

"Careful," Ed tells him. "Not a good idea to make her mad." I hear him laughing till the toilet door shuts. Before it does, I make sure I swing my arse a little. Take that, mister.

# ED

"She's swinging her arse on purpose," Leo says, laughing. "I like her."

I laugh with him till they're in the toilet and then I stop. "I don't like her. I'm going home."

"No way," Leo says. "I want to hang out with the Jazz Lady, and she wants someone for Lucy."

"I'm not someone for Lucy."

"Jazz thinks you are."

"Jazz thinks she's psychic. Jazz is delusional."

"Daisy won't hang around without the other two," Dylan says. "She's mad because I threw eggs at her head this afternoon."

The three of us think about that for a second.

"That was stupid to throw eggs at her head," Dylan says.

"Flowers work better." Leo leans across to me. "Look. We've got hours to kill before the job and three cool girls out for adventure. What's the problem?"

"The last adventure I had with her ended in hospital, that's the problem."

"So don't touch her arse this time."

"I'll try to remember that."

First piece I ever did was for her. A girl with roads and rivers and deserts running across her skin. Highways on her neck that went all the way cross-country. Off to the side of her was a guy with the hood of his car up and smoke pouring out of the engine.

I painted it a week after she hit me. In the middle of the night with a piece of white tape over my nose and two bruises under my eyes. I didn't even check behind me for the cops. "Arrest me," I was planning to say if they turned up. "Do it. Fucking arrest me."

No cops showed and I stayed there till the sun blurred the dark. It wasn't even a good sunrise. Factory smoke swallowed the color before it had a chance and the whole sky was cloudy white.

It took me months to ask her out. I'd been stalking her locker, stalking her on the way to class and at lunch. I even Googled her. Found a picture on the school website from earlier in the year when we went to the National Gallery. She was staring at a Rothko painting and I was this sad little dot in the background, staring at her. I'd been checking out the Vermeers and I came round the corner and there she was. All pearls, all eyes, all skin, all mouth.

I watched her in art while she was drawing these pictures of things tangled together. People tangled in clouds, in stars, in other people. She worked with charcoal, smoothing the lines on the page. Sometimes I couldn't see where one thing ended and another began. Sometimes the connection point was an explosion.

I kept dreaming her and me were tangled like that. Kept dreaming of this spot she had on her neck, this tiny country. I wanted to visit, to paint a picture of what I found there, a wall with a road map of her skin.

Mrs. J. paired us up for a research assignment on Jeffrey Smart and for two weeks I watched that spot. Then one day she looked up from her book and caught me making travel plans. "What?" she asked.

"Nothing," I said. "Only. I was thinking. We should see a film."

She sat there tapping on the table with her pen and my blood was tapping and I was all desperation and no cool, sitting there making plans to move to some country far off the map. But then she said yes and my chest got sucked somewhere and I walked around with this hole in me all week. I kept thinking I wouldn't make it to Friday night. That something would happen before then to mess with my luck, something like a nuclear bomb going off so there was nowhere for us to meet.

"Pretty harsh," Leo said when I called him to come get me because she'd left me in the gutter with a broken nose. She never even called to check she hadn't killed me. A date like that makes a guy wish they would drop the bomb. Right over his house.

"What do you think they're talking about in there?" Dylan asks, looking toward the toilet.

"I'll take a wild guess and say us." Leo leans back. "Girls and money, all in one night. I've got a good feeling." He checks behind him for about the fiftieth time since we got here.

I don't blame him for checking. Malcolm Dove is close to the scariest guy we know. The only guy scarier than him is Crazy Dave. He was the one who dared Malcolm to eat that cockroach. Crazy Dave only had to eat one more than Malcolm to win the dare, but he ate five just for a laugh.

Leo might say he's not worried, not about being caught by Malcolm or the police, but he is. While him and Dylan are laughing I look out the window and think about the sky in Bert's book. About how the clouds look like they're moving but they aren't. It's the same ones flicking over, again and again and again.

# LUCY

It's serious business time, so Jazz and I walk into the same cubicle. Daisy crams in too. "Is this like the cone of silence?" she asks after Jazz turns the lock.

"It's more like the cubicle of truth," Jazz tells her.

Jazz and I met like this when she arrived in year ten. I was about to lock the cubicle door when she pushed it open, slammed it shut, covered my mouth, and hissed, "Shhh."

We listened while Holly Dover and Heather Davidson came into the toilet and squealed Jazz's name. "She's not in here," Holly said when no one answered. "Let's look in the library."

"They're hard to shake," Jazz said after they left. "They've been following me since the canteen. I had a feeling I didn't want to be their friend even before they spoke. I'm psychic," she said, and looked at me looking nervously at the lock. "Psychic. Not psycho. I'm Jazz Parker."

"Lucy Dervish," I said. "So what sort of things do you predict?"

She unlocked the toilet and checked herself over in the mirror. "You've got a set of palm cards for the English talk today in the back left pocket of your jeans."

I pulled them out. "Okay, that's impressive."

"They're in the wrong order, and card number three is under your kitchen table."

"A psychic friend could come in very handy." I reshuffled my cards.

"I predict I will," she said.

We were friends from that point on. I hung with loads of different people before her. I like having friends from different groups. Some days I'd sit with the kids in my book group. Some days with the arty types. Some days I played chess. Some days I painted my nails black.

Jazz is like that too, so in the end I fell into having a best friend easily. She's the sort of person who invites herself places and she doesn't follow the rules of high school geography. She likes Scrabble and the supernatural and drama and Shakespeare and sport. She studies harder than anyone I know. "I'm eclectic," she said to Holly and Heather once, and I could see them trying to work out where she plugged in.

She stares at me tonight, hardly blinking. "Why'd you lie?"

"I didn't."

"We're out there talking about Ed, and you say nothing about him being the broken-nose guy. That's a lie, right?" She looks at Daisy.

"It's withholding the truth," Daisy referees.

"Fine. Why'd you withhold the truth?"

"You're psychic. I assumed you knew," I tell her.

She gives me the serious finger. "You can't joke your way out of this."

"I felt stupid then and I feel stupid now. I knew you'd mention it as soon as we walked over tonight, and I knew if you thought I'd liked Ed once, you'd push me to like him again, and I *don't* like him."

"But he's so cute and he's friends with Leo." She drops her voice. "Luce, when we were in the street talking, Leo's arm brushed my arm. I got static electricity *down there*."

I can't help laughing. "So go out with him. Tell me about it tomorrow."

"I want to tell you about it while it's happening."

"He'll probably think that's weird," I say.

"I want you to get static electricity too."

"I'll go rub my feet up and down on the carpet for a while when I get home. I promise."

"I remember static," Daisy says. "Dylan and I used to have it. Now he won't even come with me to Queensland for an end-of-year-twelve trip. He worked all year to get the money, and then he spent it on a Wii. Don't you want static?" she asks me.

"I do. Just not with them." I nod in the direction of the café. "I want someone like Shadow." Not someone *like* him. "I want Shadow."

"Someone you have almost no hope of meeting," Jazz says.

"Dylan knows him," Daisy says. "Him and Poet."

I've been tracking Shadow for almost two years. Kids

make up stuff about him all the time. He's dead, he's overseas, he's studying art. As far as I can tell, none of it's true. "You mean Dylan knows someone who knows someone who might know them."

"No. He actually knows them. He says so all the time. 'I went here with them, and they went here with me.' Sounds like they see him more than I do. He acts like it makes him cool." She thinks about it. "I guess it does make him a little bit cool."

I grab Jazz by the shoulders with my insides ticking fast. "I'll come tonight if we look for them. We can go to places Dylan thinks they might be. You get a night of action with Leo. I get Shadow and romance."

"Sounds like a book my auntie Glenda would read," Jazz says.

"Please, please, please."

"I wouldn't mind getting Poet," Daisy tells her. "His writing is very cool. You think there's such a thing as poetic static?"

Jazz grins. "That's definitely something that deserves investigation. Okay. I'm up for a Shadow hunt." She tries to let us out, but the lock's stuck. "That's weird."

"Is this like an omen?" Daisy asks.

Jazz unzips her boot and takes it off so she can slam it at the lock. "It's not an omen." Slam. "Tonight." Slam. "Is going to be great." Slam. "I've got a feeling." Slam. She puts her boot back on and looks at us. "Okay, we'll have to climb out of here."

She stands on the toilet seat and from there to the toilet-roll holder and then heaves herself over the wall.

"Impressive," I say, and then we hear her slam to the ground.

"Less impressive," Daisy says.

"This doesn't mean anything," Jazz calls. "Trust me. I'm psychic."

I come out of the bathroom and the first thing I see is Ed. Okay, it was a long shot, but I was half hoping he'd cease to exist while we were gone. I feel a little tingle when he turns around but I put it down to the fall I had during my toilet escape. That and the thought of meeting Shadow.

I don't look at him as I slide into his side of the booth. I'm not here for Ed. I'm here for my young and scruffy artist. "Lucy and Daisy want to find Shadow and Poet," Jazz says.

"Who?" Ed asks.

"Graffiti artists," she tells him. "They do stuff all over town."

"They call themselves writers," Dylan says.

"Whatever," Daisy answers. "We want to meet them."

"I mainly want to find Shadow," I say.

"I'm just going along for the ride," Jazz says. "I think Shadow might have some serious psychological issues."

Leo laughs, and Ed mouths "Fuck off" at him. Leo laughs some more. "We can look for them," he says. "That's a great idea."

"No, that's a stupid idea," Ed tells him. "That's the

stupidest idea I've ever heard. How would we even know where to look?"

"Daisy said Dylan knows them," Jazz tells him.

"Really." Ed stares across the table at Dylan, who looks like he's about to do a runner.

"You were lying?" Daisy asks. "Typical."

"I wasn't lying. I see them all the time. Ed and Leo have seen them, too."

Ed doesn't answer. Leo tilts his head in a way that could mean yes or no.

"So prove it," Daisy says. "Take us to the places they hang out, and if we find them, introduce us."

"He can do that," Leo says. "Right, Dylan?"

I'm holding my breath. I'm crossing everything on the inside. Lungs, kidneys, ventricles, the whole deal. Please don't let Dylan be lying. An idiot could see there's something going on between these guys, but I figure it's that Ed would rather cease to exist than hang out with me.

I imagine what Shadow looks like: paint-spattered clothes, a face that's got a million ideas running underneath it. Please, please, please.

"Right," Dylan says slowly. "No problem at all."

"Now *I* have to go to the toilet." Ed looks at Leo and Dylan. "I got a feeling you both need to go too."

"Guys don't go to the toilet together. That's messed up," Leo says.

"That's not the only thing that's messed up," Ed tells him. "So *move*."

I wait until they're gone, then I ask, "You think Dylan's telling the truth?"

Daisy checks her face in a little mirror, then hands it to Jazz. "You want me to find out?"

"Let's not ruin the mood by calling them liars." Jazz looks in the mirror. "I hate my freckles," she says, and hands it to me.

"I like freckles," Daisy says. "And I won't ruin it. I've got this special way of getting the truth out of Dylan."

"How?" I ask.

"I kick him in the balls."

"That's pretty special," I tell her, and hand back the mirror.

"Okay, let's keep our feet to ourselves and not get paranoid," Jazz says, and gives us a serious finger each. "Quick, Daisy. Spill everything you know about Leo before they get back."

"He's pretty wild. Less wild since he moved in with his gran, but still, he does some crazy stuff."

"More crazy than when he used a chain of guys' shirts to rappel out of the classroom window while the teacher's back was turned?" Jazz asks.

"No, pretty much that level of crazy. His brother Jake's been in some trouble with the police, though. I'm not sure of the details."

"Has Leo been in jail?"

"He was taken to the police station, but they didn't lay charges. Dylan never told me what he'd done. Emma, his ex-girlfriend, said he vandalized her house."

"Emma Forest?" Jazz asks. "His ex is the girl with the big . . . ?"

"That's the one," Daisy tells her.

Jazz looks at her chest. I pat her shoulder. "Guys care about personality too."

"Girls like me started that rumor." She looks at Daisy. "Why did they break up?"

"Not sure, but it was last year. He hasn't had a girlfriend since."

"No girls at all? If he's had a drought like me, then he should be easy to pick up."

"Well, no, he's been with girls. Lots of girls. Lots and lots of girls. Lots and lots and lots—"

"Okay, I get the picture," Jazz cuts her off. "What about Ed? Just in case Lucy needs a backup plan."

"I won't need a backup plan. Ow. Don't kick me."

"I don't see him much since he left school in year ten. He was going out with Beth Darling. Private-school girl. St. Catherine's, I think. She's pretty and smart. He works in a paint store now, somewhere in the city."

"Maybe that's how they know Shadow. Maybe Ed sells him paint," Jazz says.

"Maybe. Dylan never said."

"Why'd he leave school?" Jazz asks.

"Lucy."

"Me? Oh my God."

"Gotcha," Daisy says. "I don't know why he left exactly. The rumor was he cheated. Leo said that was crap."

Ed quit about two weeks after our date but I never really thought it was because of me. I figured he wasn't that interested in school. We still had all this work to do on the Jeffrey Smart assignment, but most of the time he didn't come to class. Even when he came, he sat there not talking and not writing, so I did the work for us. And then before the due date he got caught cheating and he left.

Even though I was still mad at him for grabbing my arse and for making me do all the work on the essay, I felt bad for him that day. I looked at him hoping he'd look back so I could smile, but he didn't take his black eyes from the window.

I missed him after he'd gone. I mean, it's not like the feeling he gave me stopped because he grabbed my arse. I spent the weekend after our date wishing I could stab him with my fluffy-duck pen and staring at the phone hoping he'd call. Dating is a very tricky business.

"You've got a weird look on your face," Jazz says to me. "What are you thinking?"

"Nothing," I tell her.

"Is that possible?" Daisy asks. "To have absolutely nothing in your brain? Because sometimes I ask Dylan what he's thinking and that's what he says. Just once I'd like him to say he's thinking about world peace or saving the whales or something."

"It's not possible," Jazz tells her.

"It's possible. He's not a complete idiot."

"No, I mean it's not possible to not think anything."

"That's what I tell him. And you'd know, being psychic

and all. How does that work anyway? Do you hear people thinking?"

"I get a feeling sometimes. My mum's way more psychic than me. She's got this sixth sense that she can use to track me day or night, and since the midyear exams she's had her tracker on high. 'There'll be time for dating when the final exams are over,' she kept telling me."

"So now is the time," Daisy says.

"*Officially*, the time is after my audition. But while she and Dad are in Germany at their law conference I'm counting on the different time zones messing her up. A psychic lawyer is a lethal combination in a mother."

I know Jazz worries that her mum has seen her future and it doesn't have an Oscar in it. My mum and dad and I tell her that some things can't be predicted. She wants to believe us, but I'm not sure that she does.

After they moved here, her mum wanted to send her to a private school like the one she went to in Western Australia, but Jazz begged to go to Daley High because we've got the best drama program in the city. Her parents made her a deal. She could go as long as she got good grades so she'd have a "real" career to fall back on.

The first time she met Dad, he was rehearsing his new act. She sat there watching him, blowing quiet gum bubbles. When he finished, she quizzed him for an hour about his technique, where he studied, how he supported himself, what he wanted from his career. She stayed over that night. "I'm just not ready to go home yet," she said.

"What are your parents like?" Daisy asks me. "Do they let you do stuff?"

"Yep. They're artists. They met at college and fell madly in love."

I don't look at Jazz. My parents' marriage is a subject we mostly don't talk about since I asked her to use psychic abilities to see if their living arrangement was a sign that they were getting a divorce. She took the lollipop she was eating out of her mouth. "It's a *billboard*," she said. "And I don't need psychic abilities to see it."

I went quiet and she went quiet till finally she said she was sorry. "That was a bad joke, Luce." I told her it was okay. It was okay. She spends a lot of time at my place, but she doesn't know my parents like I do. Mum says they're not getting a divorce and she has a strict honesty policy so I believe her. I asked her straight out one night while we were in the bathroom getting ready for bed. "You're divorcing Dad, aren't you?"

She grabbed my shoulders and stared at me without blinking. "For the *fiftieth* time, I promise you we're not. I love your father. I need headspace to finish my novel, that's all." She squeezed past me to get her makeup remover. "This bathroom isn't big enough to swing a cat," she said. "This house isn't big enough to swing a cat."

"So it's the cat's fault," I said. "If only we had a cat."

She rolled her eyes. "It's no one's fault. There's no fault. We're staying married. Not everyone lives like the dream you have in your head."

That did not comfort me.

I tune back in and listen to Jazz doing the wrap-up of our conversation before the guys come back from the toilet. "Okay. I need life experience tonight." She points at Daisy. "You need a new boyfriend tonight." She points at me. "You need to positively ID your new boyfriend tonight." She hands around some gum. "We've got at least seven hours to get what we want before the sun comes up."

"We should have started hanging out with each other earlier," Daisy says. "I can't believe we waited till a teacher put us in a group together." She looks toward the toilet. "They've been in there a long time."

"What do you think they're talking about?" I ask.

"I'll take a lucky guess," Jazz says, "and say us."

# POET

ASSIGNMENT TWO
POETRY 101
STUDENT: LEOPOLD GREEN

## Love in handcuffs

The girl I loved called the cops
And had me arrested
She said it was the smartest thing she ever did
Apart from dumping me in the first place

She waved goodbye
As they cuffed me
She thought it was hilarious
How I tried to wave back

The guy in the police van with Ed and me
Smelled like my dad

After a hard night on the beer
Fruity and sour

And it made me think about her
About how the first thing I noticed
Was that she was nothing
Like anything I'd had before

# ED

"We're not spending the night looking for ourselves," I tell Leo. "It's a complete waste of time."

"No, it's fun, and you are a guy in need of fun. You've been looking like this for months." Leo does something strange with his face.

"I don't look like that."

"Yeah. You do."

"I'll look like that if Daisy dumps me, and she'll dump me if she thinks I lied," Dylan says.

"You threw eggs at her head. Odds are she's dumping you anyway." I turn to Leo. "We decided. We said that we weren't telling anyone. We said it was art for art's sake. We said the more people who knew, the more chance the cops'd pick us up. We said it was you and me, no crew."

"Are you sure I didn't say it was to score girls?"

That actually sounds a whole lot like something Leo would say. "I'm sure," I tell him.

"None of us are scoring if we don't lie," Dylan says. "Go along with it, Ed. I am begging. I am on the ground begging you."

"You're standing at a urinal about to take a piss."

"Don't make me get on the ground. Do you know how many germs there are in a toilet?"

I try not to laugh but I can't help it and he knows he's got me. "Two hours and that's it," I say. "We don't tell them it's us, no matter what. We go to a few places, pretend to look, and we find a way to change the plan."

Leo grins. He's enjoying this way too much. I can see him out there now. Jazz's saying how cool she thinks the writing is and he can't hold in the secret. I look him in the eyes. "No matter what, we don't tell them."

"No matter what," Leo says.

I don't believe him for a second. But I'm still not telling Daisy that Dylan lied. Because there's something about the way he's slumped that makes me think he does care about her, even if he's not acting like it. And if he does care, then I don't want to be the one to wreck things for him. I know what it's like to want a girl. To get dragged in the dirt behind her hoping you won't lose your grip.

I know because of Beth.

When I met her I'd been at the shop for a few months but it felt like I'd been there longer. I had this sense that things were moving somewhere else but that around me they'd stopped. Every day kids walked past the paint store laughing and carrying schoolbags and I watched them feeling like I was that guy in the Jeffrey Smart painting. The one standing in a concrete world with the expressway sweeping round him. That guy could shout but his voice would only bounce around and come back to him, bounce and come back for the rest of his life.

Then one afternoon Beth came in with a couple of guys from her school. Guys in white shirts and ties, looking at me like I was a bag of nothing. While I got the paint they needed for their school banner, one of them asked, "You work here full-time?"

"Uh-huh."

"Good career move."

I took the money and passed the box across the counter and said politely, "Your choice of color really lacks style." I smiled and Beth laughed and the guy asked to see my manager.

I got Bert, and he leaned over the box and looked at the paint and said, "Ed was being polite. Your choice of color is shit."

Beth laughed even more, and it was that laugh that got me. I'd been feeling like nothing since Lucy hit me, but that laugh made me think of a wall that had something on it other than highways and broken-down cars.

She stayed after those white-shirted wankers left, wandering round the aisles, looking at me every now and then. "You should ask her out," Bert said. "No guts, no glory."

"Last time I asked a girl out, I got two black eyes. No guts, no broken nose, as far as I'm concerned."

But before Beth left she came up to the counter and said, "You should ask me out." So I did, and after that day she took the world off my chest, lifted it so I could breathe. We sat on the hill near her house and I was quiet and she didn't break any part of me. We rode our bikes home through a sea of sky where all the lights on the shitty factories were stars and the world was a place we could swim right through.

At the start there were moments, blinking moments, when we were lying together and it was warm and I could smell flowers on her skin and turps on my hands and I heard her voice with my nerve endings. Heard her with my blood and skin and I forgot things. Like how one day she'd finish year twelve and leave me behind. Like how stupid I was compared to her. I forgot because she was hanging over me, and the world was liquid and spinning and for once I was liquid and spinning with it.

I didn't think that one day she'd write me letters and wonder why I never wrote back. That she'd think it was because I wasn't into her when really it was because every time I tried to type the words, they came out wrong.

"It doesn't make any sense," Leo said, reading one of my letters. "Do you want me to write it for you?"

"No, I don't want you to write it for me."

I threw it out. I did pieces for her instead. Beth walls. All around the city. I did them thinking she'd see and know me and keep whispering those secrets in my ear. I wanted her to know I'd painted them without me having to say. There's one near the Hoover Street station. A picture of me, grass growing out of my heart while I'm talking to her. She looked at the wall but she didn't see us.

About three months ago, on the night we broke up, I painted the last wall next to it. A picture of her starting up a lawn mower. We'd had dinner with her parents, and they'd asked me what I was planning to do with my life, and the words I didn't say hung in the air. Before I left Beth said, "You're planning on doing something else, right? Other than the paint store?"

I could have told her then. I could have taken her to the wall with her face on it, the face that made grass grow on concrete. But I stood on her porch and said, "Yeah, I plan on doing something else."

There was no skin on my voice and she heard the bones in my words like I did. And I knew. One day a wanker in a white shirt would take her. A wanker who had college while all I had was a piece on a wall. So I left.

"Have you told anyone our names?" I ask Dylan before we go back out.

"I only told Daisy that I know who you are, that's it."

I put my arm out and block his exit.

"Okay, I told Raff and one or two of his mates your actual names, but that's really it."

He goes to move but I keep my arm where it is.

"Raff has the biggest mouth in the city. What if we run into him tonight?"

"We won't. He'll be hanging at the casino like always. He won't be anywhere near us."

I lean in close to him. "You say one more word to anyone and I'm telling people you cried in here tonight because you thought Daisy was breaking up with you."

"You wouldn't."

Leo's phone rings. "He would," he says as he answers it.

He talks for a bit and hangs up. "We have to swing by a party and sort out some details about the job with Jake. It won't take long."

"A party of Jake's will be hard to explain to the girls," I say.

"A party of his will be perfect. He doesn't know I'm Poet."

"And if the girls hear about the job?"

"They won't."

"They might."

Leo tells Dylan to meet us at the table. When we're alone he says, "Look. You don't have to do this job, but you have to tell me now. After we talk to Jake, that's when things'll be set." He lets me think. "I won't care. Jake won't either."

"I know." Leo doesn't get pissed. I'll write your essay, I'll forge your note, I'll kick the crap out of that guy for you, no problem. That's Leo all over, but he can't forge and kick forever. And he can't pay my share of the rent. I have to do that or Mum will say it's her job to look after me and leave school. But she's been looking after me for long enough now. "I'm in," I say, and he nods. That's it. He won't ask again.

Back in the booth Dylan tells the girls we're going to a party where we might see Shadow and Poet. Jazz and Daisy believe him but Lucy turns the spotlight on. She flicks the band on her wrist for a second and then starts with the questions. "Whose party?"

Leo steps in. "A friend of my brother's."

"So Shadow's finished year twelve, then?" she asks Dylan.

"I think they both have," he tells her.

"Did Shadow go to our school?"

"I don't think so," he says.

"You don't think so?" she asks.

"Who are you, the cops?" Dylan asks her. "I don't remember."

She's whip-smart, that's what Bert would say. Two months ago, on the day before he died, we ate in the storeroom. Valerie had packed a cold beer into our lunches, and mine loosened me up, so I said, "I got to stop falling for the smart chicks."

"I went for a smart chick," Bert told me.

I held up the beer. "You sure did. How'd you get her?"

"Asked." He took a sip. "She said yes."

"Asking's the easy bit. Then there's everything that comes after."

We leaned against the boxes of paint and finished our beers. Bert's old hands shook but no more than usual. The counter bell went and he creaked up to get it. A second later there were cans rolling all over the floor. "I'm okay," he called as I came into the shop. "Just knocked over the display. Visitor for you."

There was Beth, holding my stuff in a box, handing back the bits of me that I'd left with her. It'd been three weeks since we broke up and I'd decided it was easier to let her keep my stuff. But Beth isn't like that. She took the hard way because she wanted to check I was all right and she wanted me to have back what I cared about. A book of Jeffrey Smart's paintings that I'd lent her. A T-shirt I made in a year-nine screen-printing class. A Ramones CD.

"You should tell her you want to make up," Bert said after she'd gone.

"Only I don't."

"No guts, no glory." He finished his beer.

I stood at the counter thinking of all the ways I could get her back but every one led to the same place. Me telling her I wasn't going anywhere and her leaving me behind.

I told Bert I had to leave early and I took a can and my brain clicked off and my hands clicked on and I escaped onto the wall, a painted ghost trapped in a jar. I stood back to look at it and I knew the sad thing wasn't that the ghost was running out of air. The sad thing was that he had enough air in that small space to last him a lifetime. What were you thinking, little ghost? Letting yourself get trapped like that?

Jazz tells Lucy to relax and tries to kick her under the table. I know this because she kicks me instead. "Aim more to the left," I tell her, and she has another go. "Farther left," I say, and enjoy watching her hit the target a couple of times.

Everyone starts talking about the night. Leo flirts with Jazz. Dylan tries to flirt with Daisy while she flicks sugar packets in his face and says things like, "They bounce straight off your hair. You need to cut back on the gel." He's got stamina, I'll give him that.

Lucy looks out the window, staring at something that's in her head, the same way she did two years ago when I watched her. She hasn't changed much except now she's bunching up her hair with paintbrushes. She's still smiling like she's thinking something you want to hear.

"Why do you want to find him so bad?" I ask after a while, but she's not listening. I watch her a bit longer. "Why do you want to find him so bad?" I ask again.

She blinks and comes out of her dream. She flicks the band on her wrist. "I just do."

# LUCY

After Jazz kicks me a second time, I stop asking questions. I've got enough information for now anyway. If Shadow's finished year twelve and he didn't go to our school, then it makes sense that I've never met him. I'd know if I had, I'm sure of it. A guy like Shadow would stand out around here.

Jazz catches my eye and drums three fingers on the table. Three drumming fingers means this guy I'm talking to is gorgeous. It's not to be confused with four fingers drumming, which means get me away from this guy if you have to set my hair on fire to do it. Five fingers means I'm screaming on the inside, for good reasons. Jazz lays her five fingers on the table.

Leo's screaming good-looking, that's for sure. Five fingers to the power of ten. Tall, with a shaved head, soft eyes, and a tattoo. He's trouble, which is exactly Jazz's type.

The first guy she went out with in this state was Jacob Conroy. We were standing at the pedestrian lights one afternoon about a week after she'd arrived, and he was leaning against the fence at the train station. Jazz whistled and he turned around, put his fingers through the wire, and grinned. The sun backlit him a halo.

"I don't want to alarm you," Jazz said, "but I'm about to run across moving traffic."

"What's the rush?" I asked. "He's waiting for the three-forty-five train."

She pointed at the warning bells and they went off. "It's five minutes early."

She made it to Jacob a second before the train left. He handed her his phone number through the closing doors.

"Sorry," she said when I reached the platform. "Side effect from years of being at an all-girls school. You see someone you like in the outside world and you have to move."

"What did you say to get his number?" I asked.

"I said, 'Quick, the train's about to leave. Give me your phone number.'"

"You don't want romance?" I asked.

"The train doors didn't close in my face. I found that very romantic."

She went out with Jacob for five dates, and then they broke up. She came over that night with a tub of ice cream and a bag of Hershey's Kisses. "Comfort food?" I said.

"If I needed comfort food I'd have brought two tubs of ice cream. I'm not upset, Luce. This is what I always eat on a Friday night."

We sat in my room and I asked her what happened. "I took him to a Hitchcock film festival and he fell asleep. While he was snoring I decided we didn't have all that much in common."

"So you're like me," I said. "You're waiting for the right guy."

"Exactly like you," she said. "Except the guy who served me at the Candy Bar at the Hitchcock festival was kind of cute, and I'll probably go back tomorrow and ask him out. So I'm exactly like you if, you know, you ever dated." She passed me the ice cream. "Why don't you date?"

I showed her the photographs I'd taken of Shadow's walls. "This is the guy I want."

She looked through the walls of hearts and birds and ghosts. "So what's the problem? Ask him out."

"I would. Only, I've never actually met him. I've seen his art, just not him."

She looked at me with her serious face and handed me the last Hershey's Kiss. "We've basically just met, so I'll say this gently. Are you *completely crazy?*"

"Just out of curiosity, how would you say that if we'd been friends longer?"

"He could be a serial killer, or worse, he could be old, Luce."

"Serial killers aren't creative."

"Watch a little *Dexter* and get back to me on that."

"Seriously. What do you really think?" I asked. "Give me your professional psychic opinion."

She looked at the wall of the girl with a road map on her skin, and I could tell from her face she thought the same thing as me. "You're thinking it. Say it. Say it."

"I don't want to encourage you."

"*Say it.*"

"In the right light, from an angle and with my eyes half shut, she looks a tiny, *tiny* bit like you."

I'd been thinking that since I saw the wall. Sometimes I thought I was crazy, but most of the time I thought I was right. Somewhere out there in the darkness, Shadow was imagining me.

While we were falling asleep, I told Jazz about this drawing I love by the artist Michael Zavros. It's of a horse falling, tumbling from the sky, legs to the clouds. There's no way to right itself. It seems to me it doesn't know how it got there, or where it is, or why it's falling. The picture is called *Till the Heart Caves In,* and that title tears me open. I love the horse, how real it is; I love the fine lines of its legs and head. But that's not why some nights I can't stop staring at the picture. I can't say exactly why. Only, it's got something to do with how love should be.

"You should feel it like a horse tumbling through you," I said to Jazz.

"You're weird," she said, falling asleep. "But that's okay. It makes me seem normal."


"Why do you want to find him so bad?" Ed asks, and when I look at him, I can tell he's already asked me the question more than once but I haven't heard.

I flick Dad's lucky wristband a few times. "I just do."

# POET

**Remember love**

Remember
Love doesn't make the world go round
Sex makes it spin for a second or two
If you're lucky
So do chips, sausage rolls, and girls in short skirts
Remember
Love
Lays its fingers on your heart
And holds it
Underwater
Remember that
When the next girl smiles

# LUCY

Leo checks his watch. "If we hurry we can make the ten-fifteen train." He and Jazz walk ahead. Daisy walks to the side and Dylan shadows her, so that leaves me with Ed. He's taller than he was two years ago. His hair's still unplanned, though. There's still that space around him. He's wearing a T-shirt with a picture on it of a rabbit reading a book.

"You keep looking at me sideways," he says, "like any second I'll grab your arse. Relax. I got a girlfriend, and for your information we had a great first date."

"Maybe you learned something from how our date went," I tell him. Take that, mister.

"We didn't have a date. A date ends in a kiss, not blood and broken cartilage."

"Well, sure, if we're getting technical."

Ed raises his eyebrows, then rolls his eyes. "For the record," he says, "she grabbed *my* arse."

"Sounds romantic." I pick up a stick and pretend it's a glass blowpipe; I spin molten stars.

"It was romantic," Ed says, watching me put the stick to my lips. "She didn't give me some pop quiz and then slam me when I didn't get the answer right."

I blow a gold glass ocean. A sky. Some clouds. "Beth sounds like the perfect girl." Damn it.

"Never said her name was Beth."

"Well, all girls called Beth are arse grabbers." I try as hard as I can to act like that wasn't a stupid thing to say. Trying. Trying. Nope. No good. I make a silent apology to all the girls called Beth.

"Are all girls called Lucy nose breakers?"

"You're chattier than you were two years ago. I'm not sure I like it."

"Should I duck?" he asks.

I don't answer. I'm not used to people not liking me. At the very least they don't mind me. Although, in fairness to Ed, I haven't smacked the people I'm basing that on in the face.

I concentrate on the scenery, half-dark streets and traffic lights blinking because the grid can't take the air-conditioner surge. I use my stick to draw some things onto the world that are missing. An extra tree here and there. Some fireflies. A shadow.

"What are you doing?" Ed asks.

"Drawing."

I don't have to be a psychic to know what he's thinking. I put down my stick. I've got this hazy feeling under my lids like I'm walking through a neon dream. The heat was nuclear yesterday too, so I didn't sleep much last night. Maybe I'm asleep now and Ed's something my subconscious conjured up.

Some guys drive past and hang their IQs out of the window, which is disturbing if my dream theory is true. Leo waves. "Friends of yours?" I ask Ed.

"Something wrong with that?"

"I didn't mean it in a bad way. I'm sure guys who moon people are very smart."

He lifts his eyebrows and taps his hands against his legs.

"You have paint on you," I say.

"I work in a paint store."

"Right. Is that how you met Shadow? Does he buy supplies from you?"

"I work in a place where little old ladies come to match paint with floral quilts. You think Shadow's in there chatting to them while he buys his caps? Do you actually know anything about guys like him?"

"I know about graffiti," I say, and the words come out as if I'm an old lady saying she likes the hip-hop.

Ed laughs and it comes quick and then disappears.

"Okay, so I don't know where he buys his paint or even what you call the paint. I know I like his art. I know sometimes I'll be on a train passing a corner overgrown with grass and pollution and then all of a sudden there's this painting of an ocean. In the middle of factory land, there's the mouth of the sea."

I look across, expecting him to laugh again. He stares

straight ahead like he's trying as hard as he can to block the sound of my voice.

Tonight's going to be one of those things that seem to last forever. Maybe even longer than an after-winter wax. Leo and Jazz are talking; I hear it emptying into the street. For Jazz, at least, time'll be moving differently. For that week after Ed asked me out and before we went on the date, I felt like the world was heated glass and I was glad to be trapped.

Ed's still tapping his hands on his legs and not talking when we reach the station. Dylan stops and points to the sky. It takes me a couple of seconds to see what he's showing us, but finally I do and I want to cut it out and keep it close.

"That's one of Shadow's?" Jazz asks. "I like it."

"You'll like Poet's stuff too," Leo says. "They usually work together."

Ed gives him another dirty look. Leo grins. Dylan twitches. It feels like something's going on, I think loudly, and I know that Jazz hears my thought because she gives me her serious look and blows a chewing-gum bubble in my direction.

"Everyone stop acting weird," Daisy says. "It's freaking me out."

An announcement tells us that the train is running five minutes late, so while they walk through to the platform, I stay for a bit longer. On a wall in the distance, under a light from a tower, is Shadow's piece. It's a painted night sky that's faded at the edges so I can see the wall underneath it. Painted birds fly across, hit the line where the sky blurs into brick, and turn back. Their feathers glow. Moon birds trapped on brick.

They're not dirtied by the world; from here they look more beautiful than the real ones flying around them.

I imagine being good enough to blow glass birds that look like that. I imagine an installation with hundreds of birds the color of the moon hanging from the ceiling at waist height and spotlighted from below. People would feel as though they were in the sky with them.

I turn and see Ed watching me watching. "Come on," he says. "Train's coming."

# ED

I painted those birds a while back. Took a chance early in the morning, on the way to open the store. The light coming over the buildings was burning back the night. I didn't have to climb high. Just sat on a fence with a couple of real birds lined up beside me and did the whole thing above eye level. Balancing was the hard part. There was this one real crow laughing the whole time I worked, and as I did the last line he flew across the wall and into the sky. He circled back once, like he was saying, See? It's easy when you figure out how.

Feels like art's the only thing I ever figured out. Words, school, I never got the whole picture. I'd sit there trying to block the sounds of scraping chairs and the other kids. I'd try to make a tunnel round the teacher's voice so it came to me clear. Most days I couldn't do it. I'd hear it all and so I'd hear nothing. Like I was standing in a place where every sound was the same level and I couldn't separate the threads. It felt like I had all these doors in my head but the only ones I could open were the ones that let in sound. The ones that let in something other than noise were locked.

I couldn't have got through to year ten without Leo. He helped me with my homework and I gave him somewhere to crash and neither of us needed to know why. I went round to his place once when I was in year five. He came outside, and behind him I heard waves of music and yelling. When I think back to that day I hear the zoo. The sounds of things getting out of their cages. We didn't say what I'd heard. We walked away.

He stayed at my place that night. I was almost asleep when he started talking. About how he didn't like the smell of beer. About how he liked that my place was quiet and that my mum always checked on me before she went to bed.

"She makes me dance to old music," I said. "She makes you dance too."

"I don't mind. She never yells. She bought me a bed."

"Secondhand."

"Who gives a shit?"

I asked him what it was like to have a dad. He said he didn't think it mattered who you had as long as you had somebody good. He asked me where my dad was. I said he ran away. We passed secrets in the darkness and all the while the one I wanted to tell got closer to the surface till it was out. I told him about the doors in my head and how I couldn't finish the assignment that was due the next week.

I never told Mum what it was like for me. She figured I was good at art and not math or English and she wasn't the kind of mum to get mad at me for low marks. If I'd told her she would have worried. Or worse, gone up to the school.

Leo didn't make a big deal of it. Before he went home the next day he asked to see what I'd done, and I showed him and he fixed it for me. Didn't change anything. Just made it readable. He did that to every assignment from then on and he never told anyone.

The pieces I paint come out of my head right. No spell-check required. I hear people talking about the feeling they get when they paint stuff in illegal places. Leo says he gets this fast-moving fear swinging through him, running from his heart to everyplace under his skin. I paint to get the thoughts in me out. I paint so it gets quiet under my skin.

Lucy stares at the birds tonight. I stare at her and try to work out what she's thinking. Dreaming about some guy who doesn't exist, I guess. A guy with the ocean pouring out of his can and words pouring out of his mouth, saying things she wants to hear. I wonder what Shadow looks like in her head. What he sounds like. She turns and catches me staring. "Come on," I tell her. "Train's coming."

Train's coming and you have to go to a party to look for a guy you'll never find. A guy who exists in your head, not the guy who did that piece. Not the guy who's me.


The train belts along the line and the world outside the window rockets and blurs. Jazz and Leo take two seats on the left of the door. Daisy and Dylan take two on the right. There are no seats for Lucy and me so we swing with the motion of the train, listening to two separate conversations.

"I bet they have air-conditioning on the Camberwell train line," Jazz says. "They could at least give us windows that open."

"Kids'd stick their heads out, and bam," Leo says. "Blood everywhere."

"Who'd be stupid enough to stick their head out of a moving train?" Jazz asks.

"It'd be great if you could stick your head out of the window," Dylan says to Daisy. She licks her finger and writes *Idiot* on the glass.

Lucy laughs and I can't help laughing with her. We sway round each other, the train jolting as it shifts tracks to go south. Through the window I see flames shooting from the refinery and half a moon hanging that wasn't there before. It makes me think of a wall that Leo and me did once. A graffiti moon cut by the shadow of power lines. A *prisoner moon*, Leo wrote.

I made drawings of that moon in my book before I painted it. I wanted it to be like one of those Dalí dreamscapes Bert and me had seen at the gallery. I couldn't get those watery images out of my head and that night I dreamt of a moon locked up by shadows.

"Why'd you leave school?" Lucy asks out of nowhere.

"I was worried you'd beat me up again."

The train stops and people push on. I let a few get between us so I don't have to answer any more questions about why I left. Beth asked me once too. I told her I got a job offer and I wanted to help my mum with the rent. It was half of the truth, the better half of it. The bad half was that I got caught pulling an essay out of my pants.

It was our first in-class art essay. Until then I'd told Leo what I wanted to say and he typed it for me. But from year ten on we had to do all our work in class to get ready for year-twelve exams, so I was stuffed. "You're not stuffed," Leo said. "I'll write what you want to say, and then you sneak it in."

If Mrs. J. had been at school that day, the whole thing would have gone down different. She was sick, though, and Fennel was the substitute. He caught me taking the paper out of my pants and went off. Like me doing that was somehow all about him. He said to the class, "If anyone else's brains are in their trousers, they can come sit with me at the front of the class." What sort of idiot says *trousers*?

I didn't look at Lucy all class. I felt her staring at me, and I wanted to look back and give her some sign that I wasn't a cheat, but I couldn't think of what that would be since I'd just taken an essay out of my pants. Our date was still fresh on my face and to take my mind off her eyes I thought about paint-ings I could do. That's when I thought of the birds. They flew through my head and slammed into walls all class.

When the bell went she left with the others and Fennel shoved me toward the office. While we were walking a kid came up behind him and made this clown face and pretended to wank himself. I knew it'd be all over the school in a second. When I think back to that day all I see are wanking clowns.

Fennel got this brain wave in the coordinator's office. Told me to sit there and write the sentence "This essay is not mine" so he could compare handwriting. He'd had Leo in woodwork for years, so he knew whose handwriting it was. The essay was mine so I gave him some suggestions about where he could put it for safekeeping "till Mrs. J. comes back." He didn't think much of them, so he dragged Leo in.

"Not my writing," Leo said. "It's Ed's." He sat there with his legs stuck out and his arms crossed, staring Fennel down. We both got suspended, more for the suggestions we gave Fennel about where he could shove the essay than anything else.

Mum was sitting at the table when I got home. Her shift didn't finish till five, so I knew they'd called her. She made me a sandwich and when I'd finished eating she said, "Okay. Time for your side of the story."

I could have told her about the trouble I was having and why I did what I did, but it was too late. I'd decided I wasn't going back and I didn't want her trying to make me. "I don't like school, that's all. I want to leave."

"All the beautiful drawings you do," she said. "I thought you wanted to be an artist."

"Not all artists go to school."

"The smart ones do."

"Then I guess I'm not smart."

"That's not true. My God, every time we have an argument, I'm reminded how smart you are. Go back till the end of year ten," she said. "Then if you're still unhappy, we'll talk about other options."

I pretended to agree but I didn't go back with Leo. I knew Mum'd find out eventually but I figured I'd stay away as long as I could. I trawled paint stores for blue during the day and painted skies at night. Found a blue close to what I wanted in Bert's shop, only it was in a tin, so I had to keep going back for more.

"I hope you're not one of those delinquents who've been vandalizing the side of my shop," he said one day as he was ringing up my stuff.

"If I was, I doubt I'd tell you," I said, expecting him to kick me out.

"You get those two black eyes because you got a smart mouth?" he asked.

"I got two black eyes because I don't have a smart mouth," I said, and when he laughed, I told him about Lucy. He kept laughing till Valerie walked in and then he invited me to stay for lunch.

"I'm not bombing the side of your store with paint from a tin," I told him while we were eating. "You should stop selling the stuff in cans if you don't want people writing on your place."

"I stock it for the art studio down the road." He stared at me for a while. "Why aren't you in school?"

"I quit."

"No future in quitting."

"I got a future in art." I pulled out my sketchbook.

He looked through it slowly, creaky old hands turning the pages. After a while he pulled out his book and gave it to me.

I sat at the counter chatting to him for the rest of the day, and I came by for lunch the day after that and the day after that. By the end of the week, I was a subversive with a solid career in home decoration retail and a discount on my paint.

I went home and told Mum I had a job. That I wasn't going back to school. She came in to meet Bert before she agreed to anything. The four of us sat in the back room, me, her, Valerie, and Bert. "I'm going to tell you straight out," Mum said. "He's too smart for this job."

"I know," Bert said. "But do you want him on the street?"

There was nothing she could say. On the way home I told her I'd start paying half the rent.

"It's not your job to look after us," she said. "You save every cent you earn."

Mrs. J. visited the shop after a week too. Leo told her where to find me. She walked in and pretended to look at the paint. When I said hello, she opened her eyes wide. "Ed, what a lovely surprise. I'm glad I caught up with you. I read your essay." I didn't even have to tell her it was mine.

Bert made her a cup of tea and gave her a chair and we talked about the colors of Rothko's paintings, how they took you some other place that was all hazy sky. "You could come back," she said. "I could help, and there's a department in the school that can make things easier."

"Thanks but no thanks. I got everything I need here."

"For now," she said, and I shrugged. I knew what she meant. I was already sketching highways that didn't end, but

Bert was a good boss, and I figured that was the price I had to pay for being safe.

"You got lucky," Mrs. J. told Bert on her way out.

"You don't have to tell me," he said.


The train stops and people get out. Lucy's in the same place she was before. There's no one between us but she doesn't ask the question again. She looks out the window, maybe at that hanging moon or the shooting flames, and tells me, "I like that the skies go nowhere. In that painting. I like that the birds want to get away but they can't. I like the reflection of paint in the dark." The train starts again and I hold tight to stay steady.


The party's on Mason Street, a few minutes from the station. Leo takes the long way there, though, and I know it's to show Jazz one of his poems called "The daytime things."

Jazz says it's like a song and she sends a text to herself so she can remember the lines she likes from it. Leo grins. "See? I said you'd like his stuff."

I give him a what-do-you-think-you're-doing? look.

"It's the plan," he mouths. But he's not showing her this piece so she can think some other guy did it. Sometime tonight when he's about to kiss her, he won't be able to keep it in any longer, and he'll tell her he wrote it.

This poem's longer than Leo's usual stuff. He read it to me

before it went up on the wall. "When did you write that?" I asked him.

"Sitting at the gas station. This guy started talking to me while I was waiting for Jake."

"I didn't think it'd be so—" Jazz says, stopping midsentence.

"Henry Rollins–ish?" Leo asks.

"—good," Jazz finishes.

Leo stops grinning for the first time tonight.

"I mean, I just figured, how good can something be if the guy won't sign his name to it?"

Leo starts explaining why two guys might not want the world knowing their identities. I walk ahead and leave him to it. You got to keep moving round here.

# POET

ASSIGNMENT FOUR
POETRY 101
STUDENT: LEOPOLD GREEN

**The daytime things**

There's a guy down at the servo
With lions in his hair
Matted tails of roaring kings
A dirty song caught on his skin
He can't remember when he lost them
But he lost the daytime things

Daytime shirts and daytime ties
And shiny daytime shoes
Daytime cloudy thoughts that drift
In cloudy daytime blues

Daytime smiles from people traveling
While they ride the sunshine home
Daytime TV on the weekend
Daytime talking on the phone

Now he's crying at the servo
Midnight stumbling in his mouth
Hope slowly sliding south
A dirty song caught on his skin
Matted tails of roaring kings
Who knows where or when he lost them
But he lost the daytime things

ED

The party's spilling onto the front yard when we get there and it's only 10:45. A couple of Jake's friends call as we walk past. Leo slaps their hands and leads the way.

Walking into parties like this is like walking into haywire sleep. People move past saying things that don't make sense because they're dripping with alcohol. The house vibrates with heat and music and in the darkness people who won't re-member each other in the morning are getting to know each other real well now. Everyone here is older than us, and even though I know most of them, I do a quick check of the exits. I feel better knowing I can get out.

"What sort of party is this?" Lucy asks, staring at a group of guys who look like they walked off the set of *Prison Break*.

"The fun kind," Leo says. "Go have some. We'll find you after I talk to my brother."

"The fun kind?" Lucy shouts to Jazz. "I'm pretty sure I saw

that guy over there on *Crime Stoppers* last week." She's right. She did.

"Don't be paranoid," Jazz shouts, and drags her to the dance floor. Daisy walks behind them, blowing kisses to people she knows. The three of them weave in and out of the music and Lucy moves like she's got extra beats in her head, beats no one can hear but her. I look at Leo talking to Jake and think about using one of the exits so I can go find myself a wall and paint a girl with a bunch of wild beats.

"Ed," Leo calls, and I walk across to say hi to Jake. After we've swapped hellos I leave him and Leo to talk business and stand back with Dylan to watch the girls dance. More people crowd in, crowding out air, leaving only sweat and dark.

"You're acting worried," Dylan says. "You think something'll go wrong?"

"Yeah, I think something'll go wrong. If you got half a brain you won't get involved tonight."

"You've got half a brain," Dylan says.

"I got a whole brain, for the record. But I got bills to pay and no job."

"My mum and dad pay the bills," he says.

"Lucky you."

"No, not lucky, because they won't pay for me to go to Queensland because I spent my money on a Wii."

"So get a job at McDonald's, you idiot."

"I've got a job there. I don't have time to save that much money again. Daisy's going without me, and she'll be alone up there with all those surfer guys. You know what they want."

"A great wave?" I ask, looking over at Lucy, curving her body around those extra beats. If I painted her now she'd be made of water or sky.

"That's right," Dylan says, his eyes spotlighting Daisy. "They should get their own wave."

We watch for a bit longer. "What if surfers are her type?" Dylan asks.

"Then you're in trouble. Surfers don't wear checked shirts and iron their jeans and shave twice a day."

"I like to be neat."

"And that's fine. But you'll never be a dude."

"*Dude*'s a stupid word," he says.

I nod and while we do some more girl watching Dylan tells me about the accountancy course he's doing next year and how Daisy's going to be an architect and how they're planning to run their own business one day. He'll do the numbers and Daisy'll design the houses. "She really likes staircases," he says. "She wants to design houses that are all about the staircases."

Daisy always was one of the most interesting of the sheddy girls, I think, and I say, "You can't do all that with a prison record. Don't do the job. It's not worth the risk."

Take your own advice, Bert'd say. His voice is loud even here in the screaming music and floating smoke. There's nothing you can do for me now, Bert. You're dead and I'm buried.

I did a piece for him the day he died. Not on the side of his shop, because he would have hated that. I did it down on Edward Street near the docks where they fence off a place for people to make art.

It was nothing clever, just a picture of him with that look he wore while he was having a beer or teaching me something new. I made the painting big, though, so no one on the passing trains would miss him.

I took Valerie to see it one afternoon. We stayed with Bert's old eyes for a long time that day. She ran her hand across his face and shaggy eyebrows while I looked at the river. The water was lower than it had been for a while because rain was starting to feel like a story people told.

"I have to sell the business, Ed," she told me, and I felt sorrier for her than I did for me. "There's a hardware place in the next suburb that's been trying to buy us out for years, but Bert kept saying no. He wanted you to have it."

"I couldn't have run it anyway." I kept my eyes on the river.

"Oh yes, you could have," she said. "But I need the money. It'll be a quick sale, and they can take over almost straightaway."

I pictured the store without Bert in it and I had this thought, this feeling that there was water drowning my insides.

He knew everything about me. Knew I could barely read. Knew I was Shadow before I told him. He figured it out the week I started working for him. He came into the store with a photograph of a piece I'd done. "I was making deliveries yesterday, and I saw this," he said. "I liked it so much I took a shot to show Val."

I stared at the picture. I'd done it a few weeks back, a wall of rain carving up the bay around boats that had little mice in them.

"The water's so real it looks like it's moving," Bert said. "Like the waves are about to wash off the wall and knock you over. Val and me think an artist like this should be painting for a living."

I watched his finger moving across the lines of the waves. "It's mine," I told him.

He tapped me over the head with it. "I know it's yours. I'm having it framed. Val wants you to know it's going over the fireplace. And that if you paint on the side of anything that belongs to anyone, she's not putting beer in your lunch box ever again."

"Understood."

Before he put the shot away he said, "You know mice can swim? They panic when they get in, but they do all right."

"I'll keep that in mind."

"You do that, Shadow," he said.

Up until a couple of weeks ago I visited my picture of Bert. Most afternoons I sat there with a beer and told him about the jobs I'd applied for, about the art I'd seen. But it seems pretty clear I'm not getting another job anytime soon, so I've stopped going. Some things those old eyes don't need to see.

"Right," Leo says. "At one I pick up a van from Montague Street. At three we go to the school. Security checks are at two and four-thirty. Dylan left the window open today, so hopefully all we have to do is load the van with computers and anything else that's valuable from the art wing and then take the stuff back to Jake."

"No alarm?" I ask.

Leo pulls a piece of paper from his pocket. "All under control."

"How'd Jake get that?"

"I don't ask questions."

If I asked questions I'd ask how come we're stealing from the art wing where a teacher who's cool enough to talk to me about Rothko works. Good question, Bert says.

"I need air," I tell Leo, and slide my way through the cracks of the crowd till I get to the back door. It's blocked by a bin full of drinks so I push my way through to the front but a guy and a girl are getting right into it and I can't move past. I tap the guy on the shoulder but he's not moving unless there's a fire and even then he's probably not moving.

There's always a window, I think, and head back to the lounge room and look around. I see it close to the couch where Lucy's taking a break from dancing. She's sitting next to Gorilla, a guy who got his name because he's hairy and because his arms are so long his knuckles scrape the floor. He's grinning and moving closer and she's blocked in on all sides by a mass of bodies. I look at her and him. I look at the window. I think back to our date. She can always break his nose if he gets too friendly. I jump through, land on the grass, and turn around. Who am I kidding? I want to see it if she breaks his nose.

I rest my arms on the window ledge and watch her fighting the good fight. "So how old are you, baby?" Gorilla asks her.

"Old enough to know better," she says, looking at his arms.

"You like what you see?" he asks, and touches her leg. "You and me should do it, later."

"Did you forget to evolve?" she asks, struggling to get off the couch. I laugh because I like how she's feisty, when it's not aimed at me. I like it so much I haul myself up and drop back inside. "She's with me, Gorilla."

"I don't see your name on her," he tells me, and she looks mad and he looks like he wants a fight and I know I can't take either of them so I end this quick.

"Trust me. Find someone else. This is the one who broke my nose."

"Shit," he says. "She's all yours."

I fall onto the couch after he's gone. "You hear that? You're all mine."

She flicks her wristband. "There's a guy in the kitchen giving people tattoos. You want to go get your name on me?"

"Later, maybe."

"Did you come through the window?" she asks.

"All other exits are blocked," I tell her, and sit there trying to think of something to say. It's hard to think of small talk in a sea of couples that are slowly tattooing themselves all over each other. She can't stop looking at them and that's a bad idea at a party like this. "Don't look," I tell her.

"It's like the sun during an eclipse. I know it'll blind me but I have to look."

"You keep looking at that girl and she *will* blind you."

"What you need is a camera," the girl says to Lucy.

"No, what I need is a hose."

"Okay." I cover Lucy's eyes. "No one's looking anymore."

The girl goes back to her business. I keep my hand where it is just in case. Nice and close to her mouth.

I watch her so I'm not tempted to watch anyone else. She moves her head and feet around in time to the music. "You enjoying yourself there?" I ask.

"More than I was. It's not as bad if you can't see it."

I cover my eyes with my other hand. "You're right."

"Do you think that's someone chewing gum?" she asks.

"Uh-uh," I say. "Is that you heavy-breathing?"

"I'm trying to have an out-of-body experience."

"Do not leave me here alone," I tell her, and we laugh, and in the dark she could be a different girl and I could be a different guy. We could be two people swimming through painted music.

"What are you thinking?" she asks.

"I'm thinking this party sucks."

"I'm pretty sure that there's someone beside me actually sucking. Shadow wouldn't be at a party like this."

"This is exactly the sort of party Shadow'd be at," I tell her, and then stop myself going further because I feel her body turning toward me like the sound of his name is the sun.

"You seem to know him pretty well," she says.

"Not really." I'm glad we're hiding behind hands because it makes it easier to lie. "I catch a glimpse of him around the place, every now and then."

"I've almost seen him. And Poet," she says, and I want to say, You *have* seen him and you didn't want him.

"Oh yeah?" I ask instead.

"Yep. Tonight he was at the glass studio where I work. My boss texted me when he saw them. I arrived five minutes after they'd gone."

It's strange that I've seen that old guy but never seen Lucy once. I watch him sometimes, through the window of his studio, melting glass and changing its shape. I want to ask her what job she does for him but I don't want her to know I've been there.

"Did your boss get a really good look at them?" I ask.

"He said they were young and scruffy."

"Shadow didn't look scruffy last time I saw him." That old guy's scruffier than Leo or me.

"So how come you're not mad at me anymore?" she asks.

"Who says I'm not?"

"You're not blocking my airway."

"It's a crowded room. Lots of witnesses." I think for a bit. I'm not as mad when I'm not looking at her. Both of us stay quiet for a while and let the music weave around us. "We can't stay like this much longer," I say after three songs have gone by.

"Worried it'll get awkward?" she asks.

"More worried someone'll steal our wallets."

"Jazz is pretty keen to hang around. She said this place is perfect material for her drama audition. She's doing this Shakespearean monologue, so I don't know what inspiration she's planning on getting here."

A bottle smashes somewhere close by. "If she hangs around long enough, someone's bound to get killed," I say. She laughs again and I like it even more. Like that it's me who made her laugh.

"Maybe I'll go home," she says. "Jazz won't care now that Leo looks interested. You think he's interested?"

I like the mood she and I have got going on, so I don't want to tell her that when it comes to dating, Leo's been on the bench since Emma. I don't know exactly why. He doesn't talk about the reason she dumped him. I guess when the girl you like calls the cops, it's bound to make a guy hold back. "Maybe," I tell Lucy. "Anyway, she's got Daisy. I didn't know you guys were friends."

"It's a recent thing. You're right. Jazz's got backup. I think I'll go."

For the past ten minutes we've been on a couch hanging in the middle of nowhere, and while we're hanging, I don't think about being broke or being without Beth or being in jail later tonight. "We should go find Shadow," I say, and close my eyes behind my hand. What are you thinking? This girl broke your nose. She keeps me waiting for her answer. I think about taking back what I said and then decide to leave it out there.

"Where would we look?" she asks after a while.

No guts, no glory, Bert's old voice tells me, and I take my hand off her eyes and watch her blink me into focus. "I got one or two ideas." I tell her about the pieces at the old train yard and the skate park and I try not to act like I'm excited that she's excited.

She says she'll be a minute and pushes her way through

the crowd. I watch her talk to Jazz and wonder what I'm doing. Whatever it is I can't stop. I push my way after her, and before she can change her mind, I grab her arm and we heave with the crowd to the window.

On the grass outside I take a few breaths and while I'm doing that I see Raff and his mates forcing their way past the couple kissing at the front door. Shit. "I forgot to tell Leo something," I say to Lucy. "Give me a second."

Before I climb through the window I look back at her. She's staring at the sky like she's having a conversation with what's up there.

I find Leo on the dance floor and pull him to the side, away from Jazz, Dylan, and Daisy. "Raff's here. You need to keep him away from the girls."

"I'll take care of it," Leo says. "Relax."

I ask to borrow ten bucks. He hands it to me and says, "See you back here at two-thirty?"

The music switches to techno and the party's a moving trance. You got to get out or go with it. Say no, old Bert says, but I can't. "Two-thirty," I tell Leo. "Remember. Watch out for Raff."

I work my way through the crowd to Lucy, and before I go out the window again, I look back. I don't know for sure, but if I had to take a guess about whether Leo likes Jazz or not, I'd say he does.

# POET

DANCE FLOOR
11:00 P.M.

## Maybe

Maybe you and me
Maybe you and me
Maybe you and me
But probably not

Maybe I hang out with you longer than a night
Maybe I hang out with you longer than a night
Maybe I hang out with you longer than a night
But probably not

Maybe I forget her
Maybe I forget her
Maybe I forget her
But probably not

# LUCY

I wait for Ed outside, and for the first time tonight I see a few real stars, ones I don't have to imagine. Tiny flares burning far away. I draw around them with my finger and add a UFO or two. Adding things to the world is a game Mum and Dad and I play when we're really strapped for money. Imagine what you want, Lucy, because we probably can't afford it. I never really minded because they always found the money for the important stuff, like my glass.

Al says the game probably made me a better artist, but it was him that did that. At the beginning, even before he made me learn the names of the equipment and the properties of glass, he made me observe. "Two hours a day," he said, but I watched for longer. On weekends I came to the studio for blowtorched cheese and left just before dinner. In that studio honey balloons became Medusa suns and I didn't want to miss any of it.

Ed's taking his time, so I lie on the grass to wait for him. I draw Shadow in the sky. Dark hair, I'm thinking, scruffy but not out of control. Deliberately scruffy. I'm thinking old Ramones T-shirt. Or maybe a T-shirt that he's printed himself. I draw a speech bubble and words about art inside.

I draw Ed next to him, to pass the time. It's weird, but he wasn't as hard to talk to when I couldn't see him. Maybe he should have put his hand over my face on our date instead of over my arse. Maybe we should both have been blindfolded. Things might have looked strange, sure, but they might have turned out differently.

One of my favorite paintings is *The Lovers*, by René Magritte. It's of two people kissing. Both have a sheet wrapped around their heads. Everything's so normal in the painting: her dress, his suit, the soft blue of the walls behind them. The only weird thing is that their heads are wrapped so they can't see each other and they're kissing through cotton. Maybe it's not so weird, though. Maybe kissing blindfolded like that is the easiest way to start.

I'm a little jealous that Jazz doesn't need a sheet over her face to avoid first-date weirdness. I pushed my way through the crowd to tell her I was going Shadow hunting, and she was spinning her disco around Leo like she'd known him for years. "I'm leaving with Ed," I shouted into her ear.

"What?"

"Ed," I shouted louder. "He and I are going to find Shadow."

She pulled me from the dance floor away from the speakers. "You don't mind if I stay?"

I shook my head. "You don't mind if I go?"

"Keep your phone on. I'll text and let you know how the night's turning out."

"Do you like Leo?" I asked her. "I mean, like him more than usual?"

"I haven't known him all that long, Luce. I definitely have a feeling, but I could be getting a false reading because he's the first guy I've been close to kissing since midyear."

She waved and went back to dancing. A slow song came on, and Leo looked unsure for a second before she turned circles around him. She moved without a flicker of doubt in her body. Maybe I'm wrong but he looked flickered with doubt to me.

"What if you meet Shadow and you're not the girl in the picture? What if he's not into you?" Jazz asked me once. The thought had crossed my mind a million times. Some guys like me. Some guys don't. But I have the feeling that Shadow will be one of the guys who does.

Ed and I will find him and he'll be painting those moon birds. I don't know what I'll say first. Maybe just, "I like art."

"Me too," a voice says.

I look over my shoulder and see a guy. He's older than me, maybe by a year or two, and he's wearing a suit, but not the uncool kind. It's almost silver. The combination of sharp suit and scruffy hair really works. I spread five fingers on the grass.

"It's kind of loud in there. You mind if I sit?" he asks.

I shake my head. "I needed some air too."

He lies next to me and props himself up on his elbow. His hair falls over one eye every now and then, and every now and then he flicks it back. He catches me staring and smiles. I smile. We look at each other, look away, look again.

"Are you waiting for someone?" he asks in a way that makes me think he's asking if I'm waiting for a guy.

"Just a friend. I'm waiting for a guy called Ed. Just a friend," I say again. And then, in case he missed it, I say, "We're not together, Ed and me. We're about to go searching for a graffiti artist called Shadow. Have you met him?"

"No. But I've met Ed. He's friends with Leo, right?"

"Yep."

Some kids stumble past us, kissing as they move. "They make it look like an Olympic sport," he says. "We should hold up signs like from one to ten to grade them."

"All the people in the party are getting very high scores."

He looks at me and away again. He traces a finger along the grass, making slow patterns.

"I like drawing," he says when he catches me staring. "So why do you want to find this Shadow guy?"

"I like his art," I say, and he nods. There's something going on. I don't know what, but there's something.

"Where will you look for him?"

"The old train yard and the skate park."

"Are you going now?"

I nod. "You want to come?" I don't even feel weird asking.

"I'd like to. I can't now, though. Can I catch up with you later in the night?"

I tell him yes. Definitely. Yes. Yep. You bet.

"Great. Where are you going after the skate park?"

"Maybe Feast Café."

"Okay. So if I want to find you, it's the old train yard, the skate park, or Feast." He stands and holds out his hand. Then he pulls me up so I'm close to him. "In case I need it, can I have your mobile number?"

I give it along with my name and watch his hands key it into his phone. "I'm Malcolm," he says when he's done. "Malcolm Dove."

Dove, I think. Birds trapped on a sky. It's not out of the question that this could be Shadow. "Nice to meet you."

"Nice to meet you too," he says. I watch him walk away, get into a car, and leave. It's lucky Ed takes a while coming back. I need a little time to unzing.


"Would Shadow ever wear a suit?" I ask on the way to the train station.

"Not in a million years," Ed says.

"You've only caught glimpses of him, though."

"They were big enough glimpses to know that."

It's more awkward with Ed than when we had our eyes closed, but it's still not as awkward as I thought it might be. I guess after you break a guy's nose, semiawkward isn't too bad.

"Where's Beth tonight?" I ask.

"She has dinner with her family every Friday."

"And she won't care that you're out with me?"

"Beth's cool. And it's not like you and me are on a date."

"No. Right. Of course." I look up to the sky in the hope

that I'll feel insignificant and get a little perspective on that moment of humiliation.

"What are you looking at?" Ed asks.

Nothing that's helping. "Did you know that we're made up of the same matter as stars? We are nuclear energy exploding."

"You're not like other girls, you know that, right?" Ed asks.

"I've been aware of the problem," I tell him. "But for the record, ten minutes ago you had your hand over my face while your best friend was dancing with a girl. You're not exactly like the others either."

"Fair point."

"I think it's better to be different," I say. "Shadow is different."

"You've never met him. How would you know?" Ed asks.

"I've seen his paintings, and art reveals a lot about a person. There's this one of a girl with a road map on her and a guy with smoke pouring out of his car engine." Ed doesn't say anything. "Don't you get it? A broken-down car."

"I get it. Some girl dumped him and he's crying over it."

"I don't think he's crying over it, but if he is there's nothing wrong with being sensitive."

Ed rolls his eyes a few times.

"Careful. You look like my mother."

He rolls his eyes again.

"Okay, what?" I ask.

"How do you know he's sensitive?"

"Why are you being so snappy?"

"I'm not. Forget it. Shadow is sensitive. Let's talk about

something else. We can walk to the train yard from the station."

Good idea. Subject dropped, mister. "My bike's at Feast. We can ride there." I check my watch. Eleven-thirty.

"What time do you have to get home?" he asks.

"My parents know I'll be out all night. You?"

"I've got till about two-thirty."

"What happens then?"

He grins. "Beth."

"Right. Beth happens. I guess that means you have sex."

"Jealous?"

"No." A little. Not of Beth. I'm jealous that Ed has someone who makes him grin like that. I'm jealous that Beth has someone who grins. If Shadow turns out to be the kind of guy I think he is, then I'll be looking like Ed soon.

We'll meet and click and sit up all night and everything will tip out of me and into him and the other way around and while we're tipping the night will fade and the world will get pink and in that pinkness he'll kiss me. We'll keep taking bits of each other till we get to our center, then we'll do it and it won't feel scary or strange. "I'd do it with Shadow," I say, imagining kissing a guy who looks like Malcolm Dove.

Ed's eyebrows take on a life of their own. "Really," he says, and laughs.

"What's so funny?"

"Nothing. You can do it with anyone you want." He laughs some more. He taps his hands on his legs in time with the laughing. I have this urge to break his nose again.

"Don't tell me you haven't thought about doing it with girls before."

"I've done more than think about it."

"I meant, thought about doing it with girls that you haven't done it with." A second ago I didn't think this could get more humiliating, but maybe I was wrong.

"I've thought about it with girls that I know, sure. You don't know Shadow."

"Like Angelina Jolie never crossed your mind."

"At least I've seen her."

"Okay, so I haven't seen Shadow. I've met someone who's seen him, and that's almost the same thing. I actually think maybe I did meet him back at the party."

"Gorilla?" His eyebrows go higher than I would have thought possible.

"No, not Gorilla. Another guy I met out front. He was arty and sweet, and he wore a very sharp suit."

"Doesn't sound like Shadow to me," he says.

I turn my head to the left so Ed's clear that I'm ignoring him. He didn't have to make me feel so stupid. It's not like I said I'd do it with Mr. Darcy. Actually, I have said that before, but that was a longish time ago when I didn't have the maturity I have now.

Jazz and I once made lists of people we'd do it with. She looked over mine. "Yours are all fictional characters."

"So?"

"So you need at least one real person. Who's one real person you'd do it with?"

"Shadow," I said.

"I guess an invisible graffiti artist is one step up from fictional."

"He's visible. I haven't seen him yet, that's all."

Ed and I don't say anything the rest of the way to the station. We don't say a lot while we wait for the train. He laughs every now and then, and every now and then I think about breaking his nose.

Once the train comes and we're sitting opposite each other, I get back to Mr. Flicker of Doubt on the Dance Floor. "Is Leo a good guy?"

"We've been best mates since primary school," Ed says, resting his feet on the seat next to me.

"But is he a good guy to his girlfriends?"

"He hasn't had a girlfriend for a while, not since Emma."

"The girl with the big . . . brains?"

He smiles slowly. "Uh-huh. The girl with the big . . . brains. She was smart and funny too, by the way. And tough. I liked her."

"So why'd they break up?"

"Don't know."

I think he does know but he's not saying, which is fair enough. But I've left Jazz on a dark dance floor with this guy and want to know if she needs a heads-up about something. "So Leo just sleeps with girls since Emma?"

"He doesn't lie to them. Jazz'll know the score before anything happens."

"*If* anything happens," I say, because I don't want him

or Leo thinking that Jazz has made a decision. I don't think she has, but maybe I'm wrong, and either way I don't want Leo taking her for granted. I imagine that moment and how Jazz will feel. Nervous and excited. Hopeful that maybe she'll spend the next day and the day after that with Leo. Days falling like dominoes in her head. And then he'll tell her the score. I pull out my phone.

"You should leave them alone. Leo's a better guy than everyone thinks."

"He doesn't look like that to me," I say, and dial her number.

"Lucy," she shouts. "This party is unreal." The phone fills with music, and I know she's holding it out so I can hear. "Finally, my life is exciting. How's it going with Ed?"

"It's okay. Listen, Jazz, be careful. With Leo."

"Why? What do you know?"

"Nothing. I left you there, that's all. The plan was to stick together."

"Stop worrying about me. Have some fun." She blows what I think is a kiss into the phone and hangs up.

Ed gives me some eyebrow action. "You're mad again," I say.

"I'm not blocking your airway."

"You don't know what it'll be like for Jazz. I know what it's like to feel disappointed, after the blood and broken bones on our . . . whatever it was that we had."

He gives me loads of eyebrow action.

"Okay, it was your blood. You were probably a little disappointed too."

"You think?"

The train stops at our station and we stand at the doors but they don't open. The driver announces over the speaker that there's been a slight technical problem but we'll be on our way soon. I imagine him in the control room pressing all the buttons but nothing works to let us out. Press more buttons, I think as Ed and I stare at the doors.

Through the glass I see part of the Shadow piece hovering in the sky. "Ironic," I say, not really expecting Ed to get it.

"What, that we're locked in a train, staring through the glass at a painted sky, or because we're back where we started?"

"Well, both, I guess."

"Just because I don't know who Atticus Finch is doesn't mean I'm stupid."

"I never said you were."

"I know what irony is."

"Okay, Alanis."

"Why'd you say yes to a movie if you didn't even like me?"

"It was an accident."

"You said yes by accident?"

"No. I said yes on purpose. The other thing was an accident."

"You didn't even put me in a taxi. Do you have any idea how much a broken nose hurts?"

"You are still mad at me."

"Of course I'm still mad. You never even called to see how I was. After accidents like that, people usually call to apologize."

"That's a really good point," I say, because it is a really

good point. How could I not even think of calling? How did I not put him in a taxi? I could have called Dad. "I didn't even think of calling." I pull back from a severe eyebrow raise. "I did vomit, though," I tell him. "Which I think shows some real remorse."

He drops his eyebrows. "You vomited?"

"When I got home. Barely made the sink. I had to throw out my clothes."

Ed's quiet for a full twenty seconds. I know because I count them. Then he says, "That's a shame. I really liked that T-shirt you were wearing."

"You remember my T-shirt?"

"Up until the anesthetic I remember everything."

"I *am* sorry," I say. "Sorry that I broke your nose and really sorry that I didn't put you in a taxi."

"And sorry that you didn't call to check on me."

"I'm sorry about that too."

He leans on the wall of the carriage and folds his arms. "I'm sorry I grabbed your arse."

I can't resist. "What's wrong with my arse, mister?"

Eyebrows up. Doors open. "Got it," the driver says over the intercom.

"If Jazz is anything like you, Leo's the one with something to worry about," he says, and lets me walk first into the night, which, I have to say, I kind of like.

# POET

Dance Floor
11:30 P.M.

**Psychic dancing**

She says she knows
Which way
I'm going to move
"Next you'll be spinning around me
And heading back to where you started."

"That's proof I have no dancing abilities," I tell her.
"Not proof that you have psychic ones."
"You don't believe I can read your mind?"
I do believe her. "No."

She orbits slowly
Anticlockwise

Like she's unraveling air
Bandages
"I know things," she says.
I smell peppermint
It's too sweet in here
Too dark
Too fast
Too her

I move clockwise
Winding up
What she's unwinding

"See," she says. "You just did exactly
What I predicted
That you'd do."

# ED

"I did vomit," Lucy says, and I feel jaunty. Bert taught me that word and I like it. After my first date with Beth he drew a picture series of me being jaunty. He flicked through the pages and this little guy did a few side kicks in the air.

"I felt like that after Valerie and I started dating," he said.

I feel like doing some kicks tonight. Lucy liked me enough to vomit. "I'm sorry I grabbed your arse," I tell her.

"What's wrong with my arse, mister?" she asks, and smiles with that extra beat and I see that spot on her neck and I have an almost unstoppable urge to touch it. I don't, though, because the definition of crazy is doing something close to the same thing twice and expecting a different end.

You feel jaunty, so settle for that. Don't go asking for more. Enjoy walking next to her. Enjoy showing her your pieces and hearing what she thinks about them. Enjoy saying goodbye before you rob her school. That last thought unjaunties me a little. Bert's face floats in my head and he tells me that thieves don't deserve jauntiness.

"So we're even," Lucy says on the way to Feast.

"We can never be even," I tell her. "But we're evener."

We walk farther, and the people have thinned out in the streets so there's only a scattering left. Every now and then we step over a guy still going nowhere from the night before, determined to get there tonight. Leo never passes one of those drunk guys without giving him money, even if he only has a few coins in his pockets. He hasn't gone home since the day he moved in with his gran. "Nothing to go back for," he says, but I don't think it's that simple. I figure the few coins he flicks at the drunks in the street are his way of saying sorry he can't deal with the zoo inside his house.

"You ever notice how the night changes shape?" I ask Lucy. "It starts out thick with people and sound and then gets thinner till in the middle there's almost nothing in it but you."

"Are you often awake in the middle of the night?" she asks.

"Not often. I start work early." Or I did. Since I lost my job over a month ago, the urge to paint's been hitting me hard and I go half the night sometimes. I sleep late and spend the afternoons in the free galleries in the city. Bert and me used to go to them on Saturday mornings sometimes. We'd eat lunch in the park and talk about the art we liked. I never got sick of spending time with Bert. Never got sick of watching his old hands draw the world.

"My bike's still there," she says, pointing ahead. "You never know in this place. Sometimes things disappear."

Her bike lock is the size of a Chihuahua I had once and

I tell her it's unlikely someone's carrying around bolt cutters that big.

"I like my bike. I want it to be safe," she says, and buckles her helmet, which is blue with a lightning bolt on the side. I think about a piece I could do. A girl shaped like lightning in the sky and a guy on the ground with a lightning rod trying to catch her.

"You like that helmet too?" I ask.

"There's nothing wrong with my helmet, mister." She points at two big steps on the back of her bike.

"You have training . . . somethings? What are they?"

"Feet platforms. My dad made them for my cousin to use. Step on."

"But I don't have a cool helmet with a lightning bolt."

"Your head is hard enough."

"Funny." I steady myself without touching her.

"To the train yard," she says, and pushes on the pedals. We don't move.

"Anytime," I tell her. "You know. While we're still young and beautiful."

She pushes hard again. "You weigh a ton."

"You need me to drive?"

"I need momentum, that's all. Get off."

"You're very charming, but you must hear that all the time."

"Get *off*," she says. "I'll ride, and you run after me and jump on the bike."

"Do many guys ask you out twice?"

"Only the ones with balls."

I step off. She pedals away and I chase her taillights down the street. "Hurry," she yells. "I can't slow down or I'll lose momentum."

I run as hard as I can till I almost touch the back of her bike. "I'm not Superman," I call. She slows a bit and I do a huge leap and hit the concrete. It goes like that for a while, me running and leaping and falling and wondering how doing this proves I have balls. "It's not possible to get on this way."

"Try one more time," she says.

Once more and then that's it, I think, and run, yelling all the way like that'll give me speed. She slows a little and I leap and land with one foot on, which is a miracle. "A miracle," I shout.

"Finally," she says.

"You know, Leo's brother's hooking me up with a car when I get my license. I'm making you get in while it's moving."

"You'll drive me places?"

"If your aerobic fitness is up to it, sure I'll drive you places."

From Feast we head along Carville Street and Sycamore. Tired flats and houses float past and I close my eyes for a while and let the movement take me somewhere else, let walls drop into my head the way they do when I feel space around me. Maybe later I'll go somewhere and paint the dark that's sitting behind my eyes. A dark filled with the sounds of the city and her breathing. "This isn't bad," I say. "Feels like we're not really here."

"Don't get too comfortable. You have to get off and walk if there are hills."

"There aren't hills. I'm taking you to Shadow walls where no effort is required." I'm not showing her the hidden places. Down on the docks and inside old factories. Inside the old caravan near the skate park. "Make a right here," I say, and we roll down Pitt Street.

We pass my block of flats, but I don't tell her it's where I live. I didn't bring Beth here for months after we started going out. I liked meeting her in other places. Down the back of her garden. In the park. After hours at the paint store.

"Why don't you bring her round for dinner?" Mum asked. "Worried I'll embarrass you?"

"Worried you'll give her food poisoning."

"Leo eats his body weight here almost every night. I haven't killed him yet."

"He's built up a resistance over the years. Same as me." I kissed her on the cheek and headed for the door.

"Ed," she called. "Tell her Sunday night at seven. We'll order takeout."

Leo came too, and our table wasn't big enough so we ate on the floor in the lounge room. Mum had bought a blue rug that day because she knew I hated the carpet in our place. Beth came with flowers, and between her and them and the rug and the fairy lights, everything secondhand in the place felt almost new.

"So what are you reading?" Mum asked, because she knew Beth studied literature. *Of Mice and Men,* Beth said, and the three of them were off, listing writers they loved. Leo went on about Henry Rollins like he always does, and Mum went on about all the books she read when she was pregnant with me because there was nothing else to do, and I sat there thinking of a wall with a magic carpet. Three people on it. One guy falling off into sky. Times like that I wonder if I'm more like my dad than my mum. If he'd been there that night I might have had some company on the way down.

At the train yard Lucy clicks shut her Chihuahua lock and takes off the bike headlight. By the time I ask if she needs help with the fence, she's already over and landing on the other side. "I guess not," I say, climbing after her.

She tunnels a light road past dead carriages sprayed with Leo's and my late-night thoughts. Polar bears holding matches to glaciers, painted after Leo heard some politician say people didn't cause global warming. *You're right. It's the animals.* The earth wearing a hand-knitted jumper and a beanie. *Maybe this is why it's getting warmer?* Leo had a bit of a run about the environment and I didn't mind doing the pictures for him. I understand some of his stuff and some I don't. We walk past one of his poems, "The ticking inside," and Lucy stops long enough to read it.

"Sometimes he's like a poet," she says. "And sometimes he's more like a social commentator."

I answer by lifting my shoulders and keep walking. I never really thought about it. Lately he's been writing longer stuff but I figure he's just got more to say. Some days Leo wants to talk about what he's heard in his philosophy class, and some days he wants to sit quietly and eat a sausage roll.

"It's so close to the school, but I've never been here," Lucy says, and I tell her I stop by sometimes, to check out the pieces.

"So you like graffiti?" she asks, walking away before I answer, looking at the next carriage.

"I like some. I don't like others," I say, but she's not listening.

I look over her shoulder at a piece Leo and me did for a laugh. There's a guy holding out his thumb on a highway in the first frame and a guy picking him up in the second and the car driving away in the third. The car's number plate says *Psycho*. I laugh remembering the night we did it. Leo thought of the idea. I was just painting some guy escaping.

"See," she says. "He's funny."

"I never said he wasn't." We walk to the next carriage. "So you like him because he's funny?"

"I like him because he's clever. And you know, he and I are both artists, so we have something in common." She flicks her wristband. "I've been taking glassblowing lessons from Al Stetson for almost two years now. He helped me finish my art portfolio."

"What's that like?" I ask.

"It's cool to get an idea and make it with my hands. You know?"

"I guess," I tell her, but what I want to say is, Yeah, I know. I know all about it late at night when a thought hits me and I can't sleep till it's out and onto the wall.

"Al makes these mobiles that cover the whole ceiling, like flowers hanging from the sky. They tap against each other, and because they're different sizes and thicknesses, they make different noises. It's like a ceiling of singing flowers."

I looked through his studio window once and thought they were clouds of trumpets. I like them even more now I know they make noise. I couldn't hear that from outside. "I've seen them," I say before I think about it.

"Where?" she asks.

I cough to give myself a little thinking time. "Somewhere in the city. There's a few glass shops near the paint store."

She shakes her head. "You might have seen some of his other work, but you wouldn't have seen that one. He did it when he was just starting out, before he found his own style. He says it's a little too Dale Chihuly and he keeps it up there to remind him to be himself. I love it, but I love the work he does now too. He makes these huge vases, as tall as you. They're clear, but when the light hits them, you can see patterns all over the glass. They remind me of ghosts with engravings on their skin. Have you seen those?"

I tell her no, to be safe, but I have seen them through the window. I couldn't believe how much I liked them because usually it's the color of something that gets me.

I think about how very cool it would be to exhibit somewhere. I know most guys who do walls say they don't need a gallery, but I wouldn't mind a white room with my pieces hanging in it. Bert and me went to an exhibition of Ghostpatrol, this street and gallery artist. "You could be here," Bert said. I told him he was dreaming. He told me dreaming's the only way to get anywhere.

She stops in front of a picture of me, standing in a thin night. I painted it not long ago. Everything around me on the wall is a sliver. Skinny streetlights shine skinny beams. She stares for a while but she doesn't figure it out.

"So what's your folio?" I ask.

"It's made up of twenty memory bottles called *The Fleet of Memory*. They're sort of part boat, part bottle, part creature," she says, and hands me the bike light. I shine it on her so she's a mixture of ghost and dream. "I blow them up and swing them out," she says, and I don't know exactly what that means, but it makes me think of a wall where glass balloons take off from her lips.

She pulls out a stub of charcoal from her pocket and draws around the picture of me. Charcoal on that surface will barely last the night and I know I'll come back tomorrow and make her pictures permanent.

Some of her bottles are smooth half-moons, curling at one end so they can hook onto other bottles. Some are misshapen suns that narrow and rise into one long, thin line of light. Some open at the end like trumpets, some in a twist of curls that make me think of a circus.

Her fingers smudge the lines, and I'm back at school, watching her draw tangles. I think maybe these bottles started from there and I want to ask her if they did, but I don't.

After a while she stands back and we look at the shapes circling me in the thin night. My piece looks better with them on there and I try not to show what I'm thinking. That her work is strange and cool and beautiful, like her.

"They're what I imagine memories would look like," she says, "if you could see them. That's weird, huh?"

"Yeah, but you're weird," I tell her, and think of a wall I want to do of a guy with an ocean inside him. I want to paint her boat bottles sailing through his seas.

"Some of the bottles are memory itself." She runs her hand over the circus. "You know how sometimes a moment isn't a word in your head, it's a smell or a sound or a shape?"

This night will be a bird flapping on a wall. "I guess."

"Some are clear glass, and more regular-shaped." She points at one that looks almost like a normal bottle mixed with a canoe. "They represent the things you don't remember. Some of the bottles are filled with things. Al gave me the idea for those. When he was a kid, he made those ships in a bottle."

"What's inside?" I ask.

"Mostly stuff I remember from when I was a kid. Like in one there's a tiny cape and a wand to remind me of when I was ten. My mum sewed costumes for me and her so we could be in Dad's magic act. He's a comedian, but sometimes he does kids' parties for extra money. Mum and I got into the box and Dad tapped it, and when he opened the curtain, we were gone, and when he tapped it again, we were back."

"So, what, you went out through the back?"

"That's the thing," she says. "The way I remember it, we really did go somewhere. I mean, I know now there was a trick to it, but back then Mum knew what it was and I didn't. The way I remember, Dad made it happen."

"My dad was a magician too," I tell her, looking at those empty bottles. "Got my mum pregnant and disappeared."

"Oh," she says with this strange look on her face.

"Don't worry. He did it before I was born. I never even met him." He's in this yard, down the back somewhere. A wall with a man-shaped hole painted on it.

We walk down the rest of the train yard, and she talks about the colors of Al's studio and I want to leave here and go there with her. To that place where the trumpet garden hangs from the roof.

Every now and then we stop to look at something Leo wrote or I painted. The last painting she stops at is one I don't want her to see. There's nothing funny about the white ocean. There's a rhythm in the paint, like the water's trying to catch its breath. *The disappointed sea*, Leo's written underneath. He used a font he called Empty, and the words look like exactly that to me.

"You ever feel like that?" Lucy asks. "Just flat to the edges?"

I think about the night I painted it. A week after Bert died. A week of walking into the storeroom, expecting him to be there. Seven full beer bottles lined up on the windowsill because Valerie kept putting them in my lunch but I couldn't drink them without him.

I don't want to get into that tonight. "What I'm really disappointed about is that *Veronica Mars* didn't go past a third season," I say. "And that Butterfingers don't come in king size."

"They do now."

"Well, that's very good news."

"I want Reese's peanut butter cups to come in king size, but it's never going to happen," she says.

It does seem strange, now that I think about it. "You're right. Why don't they make the others bigger?"

"It's a mystery."

"You could buy three and melt them down and freeze them," I say.

"It'd be messy."

"It'd still be chocolate. It'd still taste the same."

"I guess. But I like my Reese's neat, with the peanut butter *inside*."

"You've got a pretty hard-line stance on the inside-outside thing."

"I do," she says, and I like that she can talk about art and chocolate in the same conversation. I like the idea of her bottles. Memories that are nothing but a strange shape floating inside of you, memories that are nothing but empty bottles. And the good stuff, glassed in so it can't float away.

We leave the painting and head back toward where we came in. "I always wondered how they got those ships inside the glass."

"Al showed me how," she says. "You make the bottle first. Or you buy it. The ship goes in after. You build it outside, with collapsible masts. You lay a sea of putty in the bottle, and then you slide the ship through the neck and raise the sails from outside. That's how I got my memories in there. I made them small and collapsible. I think I liked those bottles better when they were still mysterious, before I knew how they worked."

She's got this chip in her front tooth and I think about running my finger along the edges of it. But then I think about her finding out I'm Shadow. I think about her being disappointed because I'm a guy going nowhere, not a guy who's sensitive and smart and funny. I think about her going to college and making glass and me staying where I am spraying walls and scraping rent.

"I can show you how to get the ship in the bottle," she says. "If you want."

"I don't know. Seems like a lot of trouble for a boat that's going nowhere."

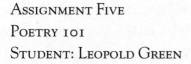

**The ticking inside**

On the inside of him there's a wire fence
And past the wire fence is a dog
And past the dog are thieves
And past the thieves
Is a gang of bad dreams
And past the dreams
If you can get past the dreams
Are the things that make him tick
Tick, tick, tick

# LUCY

Ed and I walk through the carriages, and I'm in a Shadow world that I didn't know existed. I imagine him here alone, painting in the blush of light from the next street, and I want to find him even more. Every now and then I think he's here because in the dark Ed looks like a shadow that someone else is casting.

I tell Ed the things I want to tell Shadow. I tell him about my folio, *The Fleet of Memory*. It started from the tangles I drew in class. While I was watching Al and Liz and Jack work, I'd draw the hollow I get inside when I see a moon I could drink right out of the sky, or the spinning yellow of the sun that happened between Ed and me that day he asked me out.

Those tangles shifted and changed, like the glass Al made, and eventually I had a page of bottles that looked kind of like boats floating on an ocean. After I'd spent two weeks watching and drawing, Al asked to look at my sketchbook. "They're like a fleet of memories," he said, and when he did, I knew that's what they were.

They were all the things I thought and all the things I remembered. I liked the idea that in the canals under my skin, these strange shapes were moving through, slick with color.

"You'll do these for your year-twelve folio," Al said that day.

"They're not a little weird?" I asked, turning the page around a few different ways.

"Strange things are sometimes the most beautiful," he said. "These forms, they'll look like they've risen from the center of you."

I tell Ed how I blow them, swing them out, and blow them again. How I've made them look like a mix of bottle and boat and creature. I push my memories out of me, and the glass takes on their shape.

I draw them around Shadow's picture of a boy standing in an empty night. Strange and beautiful bottle boats that float through the ocean of me now float around him on that wall.

All of them are curved underneath. Some open at the end like regular bottles with a flat round lip. Some open into curled glass designed to hook onto other boat bottles. All of them sit on a sheet of blue glass.

Ed watches me sketch, and every now and then I look back at him, but I can't tell what he's thinking. I say the boat bottles are what I imagine memory looks like, and he says I'm weird, but then he walks close to the wall and stares at the shapes.

There's too much quiet, so I fill in the quiet with the reasons I made the fleet. Sometimes a memory is a thing that can't be explained using words. One of the bottles I've made is a twist of deep blue; I remember feeling like that one Christmas Eve when I was a kid.

I explain how Al gave me the idea for those bottles with things in them. "When he was a kid, he made those ships in a bottle."

Ed asks me what's inside some of them, and I feel funny telling him because he might not get it. The memories that are in there are my most important ones, so some of them are from when I was a kid, the things I remember about Mum and Dad before the weirdness of the shed.

In one bottle is a clay fish. It's small enough to fit through the bottle's neck because some things you can't collapse. It's in the memory fleet because we used to camp at Wilson's Promontory. Mum would pretend to cook what Dad had caught, but really they weren't big enough, so she bought dinner from the fish-and-chips shop and we all pretended that the fish had come from the ocean. Dad pretended so well I was never really sure if he knew the truth.

In another bottle there are a few things stuck in the putty: the corner of a page from Mum's manuscript, a tiny piece of my glass, and a joke from one of Dad's acts. "Art is more important than money, Lucy," Mum said when I told her about Al's offer to teach me. "We'll afford it somehow, don't you worry about that."

I tell Ed about Dad and the act that made Mum and me

disappear, and he says, "My dad was a magician too. Got my mum pregnant and disappeared."

He says it doesn't bother him but his face looks like one of those clear-glass bottles and I know that it does. So while we walk through the yard I tell him about the colors of Al's studio, the flowers hanging from the ceiling. Al showed me how to make those flowers. I turned the pipe while he blew on the end, and we watched melting glass become petals.

Some days I don't want to go home from the studio. I stay with those flowers because the light shining through them makes the studio a pastel sky and the shed where Dad lives is falling down. He tapes plastic bags on the windows to keep out the insects and rain.

We move through the paintings, to the middle of the yard and farther, till there's nowhere to go but the last painting. *The disappointed sea,* Poet's written. I feel like that when I see my dad walking out of the shed in the morning in his dressing gown and slippers, carrying his little toilet bag. "You ever feel like that?" I ask. "Just flat to the edges?"

I don't know what I expect Ed to say but I don't expect him to talk about *Veronica Mars* and Butterfingers and Reese's peanut butter cups. I like that he can talk about art and chocolate and TV and neither of us goes quiet trying to think of things to say. At least till I offer to show him how to make a ship in a bottle and he tells me it's a waste of time. Nothing about art is a waste of time. "It's the time wasting that gets you somewhere," Al says.

Shadow would have known that. He would have said yes,

and we'd have headed back to Al's to see my folio and made collapsible ships that sail on putty. I imagine him, in his silver suit, leaning over his ship, gently bringing up the sails.

"You don't have to look for Shadow with me," I say when we get back to my bike. "You can leave. Or I can ride you to Beth's place if you want." I put on my helmet.

He shrugs and says, "If you want you can drop me at the station." Then he crouches like a runner. "Okay, I'm ready. Go."

"You're making fun of me."

"Uh-uh. I'm excited by the challenge."

He looks so stupid that it cancels out my stupid, so I give in and ride, and he runs and gets on the bike after only two tries. "That was much easier," I say.

"You run next time. We'll compare definitions of easy."

Mum says be careful of boys who never take anything seriously. Dad says a boy needs a good sense of humor to get through his love life. Jazz says my dad must need a sense of humor to get through his love life if he's living in the shed.

"So who else's nose have you broken since mine?" Ed asks.

I make like I'm counting. I don't want to tell him that I've had exactly no dates since him. I've spent my time looking for Shadow. Which could, to some people, Jazz says, look a little pathetic.

"That many, huh?" Ed asks.

"Okay, well, David Graham asked me on a date. I said yes, but I backed out after I heard him say in art that anyone could paint the shit he saw at the Picasso exhibition. A guy who thinks that is stupid."

"That is stupid. *Woman with a Crow*. Not everyone could paint that."

The night wheels past us, lights and roads and trees. "You like that painting?" I ask. "You know that painting?"

"Don't sound so surprised."

"I'm not. I just thought—"

"That art's a secret club only you and Shadow get to be in?" Ed finishes my sentence.

"No." Maybe. I don't know. I am surprised. If he really liked art so much, how come he didn't say something on our date? How come he quit school in the middle of our Jeffrey Smart assignment and left me to finish the work by myself? "Did you go to the exhibition?"

"Bert and me went to see that painting. Bert liked how it looks as if the woman in the painting is in love with a bad bird. 'In love with the bad times,' he said."

"Who's Bert?"

"My old boss at the paint store. He died two months ago. Heart attack in aisle three."

"That's awful."

"Better than a heart attack in aisle four, which is where they keep the floral wallpaper. Bert hated that aisle but it was the money-spinner. He died looking at the deep reds."

"I guess if you have to go, it's best to see something beautiful on the way out. Do you miss him?"

"He was a good guy. Paid me more than he could afford but I didn't know that till after the funeral. He taught me stuff. And he drew the coolest things. Stop for a second."

"If I stop pedaling, you'll have to run again."

"I know. Stop for a second."

I do, and he gets off and pulls a book out of his pocket. The pages are bent, and it's dirty around the edges. We lean on someone's fence and he moves in close. "Look." He flicks the pages, and a little guy does a couple of kicks in the air.

"That is the coolest thing."

Ed flicks through all these animations. Two guys drinking beer. A dog rolling over and playing dead. A guy at a counter serving a woman. A man on his knees proposing. "That's Bert asking Valerie to marry him," Ed says, and I like the little smile he gets when he says it. I like the way he holds the book. Like maybe all those drawings add up to love.

The last one is of a guy in a car waving and driving away. Ed hesitates over it. "He drew this one the day he died. That's me. With my driver's license."

"How do you know it's you?" Ed holds the tiny picture next to his face. There is quite a likeness. Something about the eyebrows. "Plus," Ed says, "Bert was quizzing me so I'd pass my driving test." He flicks the pages, and a guy smiles and waves a license out of a car window. "I failed once but Bert was already making plans for me to re-sit the test so I could drive the delivery van."

"Everyone fails at least once."

"That's what I hear," he says, and we look through the book again. He stops at the one of Bert drinking beer in the sun and flicks the pages to make him raise his glass a few times. "What do you think happens after you die?" he asks.

"I'm not sure. Jazz says we come back and get a second chance at things."

Ed looks around him. "Hope I don't come back to this place."

"You don't like living here?"

"You do?" he asks.

"I like how it looks at night. I like the bridge, all those car lights moving in the dark. Mum and Dad and I used to drive over it because Dad likes the view."

"That's a little strange," Ed says.

I nod. And that's not the weirdest thing about us. We haven't driven over the bridge together for a while. Dad and I still go sometimes. He took me over to get an ice cream in South Melbourne after I found him nailing a number on the shed. "132*a*?" I said. "We're all 132." I pointed at the house.

"Yeah, but the pizza delivery guy keeps getting confused. Don't frown like that, Luce," he said, and we went for a drive over the bridge, and the world that was dirty during the day spread speckled and polished beneath us.

"When are you moving back in?" I asked.

"Soon," he said.

"Jazz says you're getting a divorce."

"Well, Jazz is wrong. I'd tell Jazz if that were going to happen. Would I be living on the property and spending time with your mother every day if we were getting a divorce?"

"No," I said as we drove past billboard signs that were disappearing too quickly to read.

I had Dad drop me at Al's that night. I sketched a new ship in my fleet, a blue one, curved like half a sky. Over the next few weeks I worked on it. I put a bridge inside, built it out of toothpicks and matches. I crushed glass into black putty to make it look like lights in the night. I bought a toy car and made *three* tiny people to put inside. That bottle took me the longest time. Al couldn't believe it when I'd finished. "It's as if you've shrunk the world and glassed it in."

Ed closes the book, and we watch the street. "Do you ever hear from your dad?" I ask.

"Uh-uh. Mum said they had the biggest fight before he left. She was fifteen and he was sixteen, and after she told him she was pregnant he left so fast he made a dad-shaped hole in the wall."

"Do you miss him?" I ask.

"You can't miss a hole." He flicks through his book. "Mum barely remembers him. I know he grew up around here. That he didn't like school. That his favorite band was the Smashing Pumpkins and he met Mum in a mosh pit at one of their concerts. His first words to her were, "Today is the greatest day I've ever known," which is a line from a Smashing Pumpkins song. I think that makes him a wanker. She thought it made him cool, but in hindsight, she says I'm right. His last two words to her were 'fuck' and '*fuck.*'"

I laugh and then stop. "Sorry. That's not really funny."

"I don't care that he left. Mum's enough. We never had a whole lot of money, but she shopped in old stores and made the places we lived in look okay. She's got a way of finding things cheap when we need them. Old tables and bookshelves. Lots of vinyl albums. My middle name is retro."

"Really?"

"No, it's Phil. Edward Phil Skye. Philomena was my grandma."

I try really hard not to say it. I wait for a full ten seconds at least. "You're named after a woman?"

"You're very sensitive, but I'm guessing you've heard that before. I don't mind having her name. She looked after me while Mum finished year ten, but then Grandpa died and she got sick, so she went into a home. She left me her Pez collection when she died. Mum added to it all the time. She used to look around in secondhand stores and find me these old ones like Popeye and Space Man. I must have at least a hundred of them."

Ed says all that so quickly. But if you slow it down and think about it, his mum lost her mum and dad and had to leave school and look after a baby all at sixteen. Plus, he lost his dad. I want to say something about it, but all I can think of is, "There needs to be a Pez Picasso." Ed's right. I'm not really all that sensitive.

"That sounds like a good idea," he says. "But I wouldn't feel right eating candy from the master's neck."

"Maybe the candy could come out of his paintbrush."

"Maybe," Ed says, and we stop talking for a bit while a group of kids walks past. Ed watches them and I watch him. I like the way he talks. It's the right amount of strange. He should have talked more on our date.

"What was your dad's name?" I ask after a while.

"John. Mum can't remember his last name."

"Imagine loving someone enough to sleep with them and then forgetting their name," I say.

"She didn't love him. You don't have to love someone to have sex with them."

"I know that," I say, trying to act like I'm not embarrassed for thinking love and sex are the same thing. I know they're not, but I want them to be close enough to at least brush each other as they pass. "It'd be nice, though. If it happened that way. If people stayed together."

"Go visit Leo's parents. Nothing nice about them staying together. He says I'm better off with one good parent."

"Daisy said he lived with his gran."

"You guys did a lot of talking about us while you were in the toilet."

"Like you didn't talk about us when *you* were in the toilet."

"We talked about the dangers of hanging out with you," he says, and it actually has a ring of truth to it.

"That's pretty much what we talked about," I say, which has a ring of truth to it too. "Daisy said Leo had maybe been in trouble with the police once."

"No charges were laid. Mum says Leo's a good guy. Just sometimes he's working undercover."

"But his parents aren't good?" I ask.

"They drank too much, I think. He hasn't lived with them in years." End of story, Ed means, and that's fair enough. I might think my parents are weird, but I get to see Dad every day. I *want* to see him every day. Sure, I had to read him the health regulations so he stopped using the lawn as his early-morning bathroom, but it was a fairly minor fault.

Ed's quiet for a while longer, then his laugh breezes over me. "What?"

"Nothing. I was just thinking. You hit me because you wanted Mr. Darcy and I wasn't him."

"You know who Mr. Darcy is?"

"I exist, therefore I know who Mr. Darcy is. Beth studied the book in lit this year. She made me watch the film with her over and over. She knew it back to front, that and all her other texts."

"She sounds smart." I try to make that comment seem casual, but weirdly, anything I say about Beth comes out of my mouth dressed in a full-length ball gown.

Ed looks across at me, and I can tell he's heard the weirdness in my voice, but he's not sure why it's there either. "She *is* smart." He flicks through the book again, speeding up people and slowing them down. "Smarter than me, that's for sure."

I watch his flicking hands. "You're smart."

He gives me a little eyebrow action again. "How would you know that?"

I think about it. I know he is, I'm just not exactly sure how I know.

"See," he says before I can answer. "You don't know."

"You're funny, which you can't be if you're not smart. Dad says it's harder to make someone laugh than it is to make them cry."

"Because you can always punch someone to make them cry."

"Exactly."

"So would I have seen your dad's comedy act?" he asks.

"Nope. I mean, not unless you hang out at late-night clubs

where they have open-mike nights." I look at Ed with his old jeans and steel-capped boots and think about him skipping class with the sheddies. "You probably do hang out at late-night clubs."

"I told you—I go to bed early. I have to open the shop at seven-thirty in time for the trade guys and to get deliveries. Bert didn't get there till eight-thirty so I always had to be on time." Ed's hands tap on the book. "I was never late," he says, and I get the feeling he's not talking to me, so I don't interrupt. We lean on the fence and watch the street. "What's the time?" Ed asks.

"Twelve-thirty." The night's thinning out like he described before. There are a few people waiting for the last tram, some taxis moving past. Ed and me. "Don't Beth's parents care that you're meeting her so late? Or early, I guess."

"I don't knock on the front door," he says. "We have this place, down the back of her garden. There's a huge tree that blocks the view from the house. I get in over the back fence and meet her behind it."

"Romantic."

"Till her dad catches me. I got my escape route all worked out, though, so no one's getting hurt."

"Except Beth," I say. "Sure, you get over the back fence, but you leave her standing there."

"Beth can take care of herself."

Thinking about him jumping the back fence makes me think about him leaving, and that makes me wonder how long we can stand here till we run out of things to say. I shuffle around so he knows I'm okay with him going if that's what he feels like doing.

"You flick that band on your wrist a lot," he says. "Some guy give it to you?"

"Yep. Some guy." I flick it. "It's my dad's lucky band. Lucky things happen to anyone wearing this band."

"So how's his luck since he gave it to you?"

I think of him sitting on the deck chair outside the shed. "His luck's okay. You know, you can leave. If you want."

"That's twice you've told me that," he says. "What if I don't want to go?"

The heat rising from the takeaway place nearby makes the air look like satin, like I could touch it if I wanted, and I concentrate on that instead of looking at Ed. "Where do you think Shadow is right now?" I ask, because I can't make my mouth say that it's okay if Ed doesn't want to leave.

"Waiting for you to come and do it with him," Ed says, and I don't have to look to know that he's smiling again.

"It's not like I'm searching for the tooth fairy or something." I get on the bike. "Shadow exists. And I don't know that he'll like me, but I just want to meet one guy, *one* guy, who thinks art is cool. Am I asking too much to meet someone who can talk and who paints and who has a brain?"

He gives me his standard eyebrow action.

"What?"

"He'll only be all those things until you meet him. Then he'll be like every other guy. And for your information, a lot of guys have brains."

"Get ready, mister. I have a feeling you're going to need a run-up."

"Uh-uh. I'm not running after you anymore." He balances on the back of my bike and pushes off with one foot to give us momentum. "Pedal now. *Now*. We've been doing it all wrong," he says.

We take off along the side streets and Ed puts his hands on my shoulders and the small circle of bike light pearls the road ahead. I think of those Bill Henson photographs Mrs. J. showed us, of teenagers in the night. When I looked at them I felt like someone got it, like someone saw what it was like to be bare skin shining in darkness.

"By the way," Ed says as we ride, "I think art is cool."

ED

I keep my hands on Lucy's shoulders even though her skin's burning me all the way up my arms. I don't mind the feeling. The road rolls by and my brain rolls with it. Thoughts spill from my head to my hands. They'll tap till I paint the thoughts right out of them. "I think art is cool." That's thought number one.

Thought number two is about my plan to jump the fence and leave Beth if we ever got caught in her backyard. It made me feel better knowing I wouldn't have to explain myself to her dad but I never thought of what it'd be like for her, staying behind.

Thought number three is about me telling Lucy that I didn't care about Dad leaving. I don't. But sometimes I wonder things. Like if it would have been easier for Mum if he'd stayed. Like if I'm the same as him.

Thought number four is all about Lucy and her flicking band and shuffling feet. She's always moving like she's got somewhere to be. I want her to stand where she is for a while. Stand still and talk to me about the strange things she's got going on in her head, since I just unloaded on her half the strange things in mine.

Thought number five is about her saying she'd do it with Shadow. It goes without saying that I wouldn't mind doing it with her, but that's not likely since as soon as she knows I'm Shadow that offer won't be on the table anymore. What we have here is a catch-22. I can't do it with her till I treat her right and tell the truth. And if I tell the truth and treat her right, then she won't do it with me.

"You got to treat a woman well," Bert said one day when we were unloading paint.

"I treat Beth okay," I told him.

"You got to be honest," he said. "Valerie says all she wants from me is some goodness and the truth."

"I can't tell Beth about me being Shadow. She'd get up-tight about me doing something she thinks is dangerous."

"That's not why you won't tell her. You won't tell her because what's on that wall is what's going on in there." He tapped my head.

"Take a left," I tell Lucy. "That piece is here." It's the one I painted after Beth gave me back my stuff. The ghost in a jar. Lucy does a quick search for painting shadows before she looks at the wall. I stand behind her, watching her watching my work. I feel like I'm shedding skin, feel like if she turns she'll see a skeleton man behind her and then she'll know.

But she doesn't. She looks at me and then back at the wall. "He must feel like that sometimes," she says, and I don't say anything because anything I tell her will give me away. "Like he's stuck somewhere and the lid's on tight."

The lid's on tight, the lid's always on tight, and there's nothing that can open that jar but smashing. That's how I felt sometimes, in the shop after I left Beth. All I wanted to do was paint. But then Bert died and I was out of the store and into a worse place because I didn't have any money coming in. "He's got airholes," I say, pointing at the top of the jar.

"That's the worst bit." She wheels the bike around so the light hits me. "His paintings are hardly ever hopeful, are they?"

"Maybe he painted that on a bad day." I don't know if I ever feel hopeful when I work. I feel a high kick in and relief. Maybe that's hope.

I look across at the line of the city. The nights are mean in this place, full of smog that eats stars. "Who does feel hope round here?"

"I do," she says. "Al offered me a job as his assistant. I'm going to college next year."

"Maybe Shadow's not going to college. Maybe he doesn't even have a job."

"But he's good," she says. "Really good. And he makes stuff better, just by painting. I was sitting at a bus stop one time, getting annoyed that I was running late, and then I noticed this small piece by him across the road. This bug looked at me with eyes that said, Can you believe this? I've been waiting here for half an hour. The picture didn't have any words. It didn't need any. The eyes were enough."

"How'd you know it was his?" I ask her. "If there weren't any words?"

"I know," she says, and because of the way those words feel I keep my eyes on her hands.

"This blue's from his sky," she says, turning them over so I can see. "I brushed against a piece of his earlier. A guy who paints like this is doing something. He's not sitting around."

Listening to her, I feel like I did when Bert talked about where I'd be ten years from now. "Famous artist," he said, and I felt like I needed to run but my skin wouldn't let me. I had this urge to throw cans at the windows so I could hear a noise that sounded like escape.

"We should go," I tell her. "It's not safe to stay in one place at night."

She doesn't move. "What does he look like? In the glimpses you've had of him?"

"Guys don't really check out what other guys look like. I guess he's tall. Dark hair. Muscles. Very big muscles."

"But you've never checked him out," she says.

"It's hard to miss this guy's muscles."

She still won't drop it. "But what does he look like?"

I shake my head. "I don't know." She stares at me and I search around for a word to get her off the subject. I grab the first one that comes into my head. "Lost," I say, without knowing that I'm going to say it. "I guess. I don't know."

That's enough for her, for now, and she gets on the bike. I push off, but I'm having real second thoughts about going farther into the park. Leo and me can be out in the dark because he's a giant and used to fighting. I know some of the other crews and they're cool, but not everyone out at night is friendly.

Lucy won't listen to me though and we go farther into the park, on paths I'd rather not go with her. Twisted ones that lead to the center and make me think of paths curving into the sky and stopping. It's hard to see where we're headed from where I'm standing. For all I know we could be on a path that ends and we fall into who knows what. Leo and me have fallen down a few hills around here before.

"Maybe we should go back. Some of the path isn't fenced. There's a pretty big drop round here somewhere," I tell her. I want to go to Feast and have something to eat. Go somewhere with lights and other people. Somewhere far away from the things I paint.

"We'll feel gravel if we go off the path, won't we?" she asks.

"I guess."

"Then stop worrying."

"Easier said than done," I tell her.

"You have to let your mind go somewhere else," she says. "Let it drift to places you want to be. When I don't want to do something, like give a talk or take a test, I imagine that

I'm in Al's studio, blowing glass. I'm turning the pipe, and I'm breathing out and making something grow from my breath."

Something about her voice puts me at a wall, in the night, darkness all around, with a world I made in front of me. We both stop worrying.

That's when we fall off the path.

# LUCY

I might be jinxed. It's either me or Ed. That thought occurs to me as I'm sailing over the edge and down a hill on my bike and I feel Ed bouncing off the back. It sounds like he's rolling fast, and I hope he's not out in front of me somewhere.

It would have been better for both of us if he'd held on tighter. Without his weight my bike gains momentum and I move so fast I think I'm going to die. "Shiiiittttt," I yell, and hold tight to the handlebars. My arms and legs and face cramp up. Uneasy rider, coming through. I go over a bump and keep moving. God I hope that bump wasn't Ed.

I get this moment of clarity as I'm racing, a spark that hits me out of nowhere. If Dylan knows Shadow, and Dylan and Ed are good friends, why doesn't Ed know Shadow better? The moment of clarity doesn't go any further than that because smacking into a tree in the middle of the night will knock clarity right out of a girl every time.

I take off my helmet and lie there, catching my breath. "Ed? Are you alive?"

"Yes," he says from somewhere close by. "And that's genuinely surprising since your bike went over me about halfway down. You're a very dangerous girl to date."

"We're not on a date."

"Lucky me. I might be dead if we were. Are you hurt?"

I do a quick check. "Nope. The rocks cushioned my fall. Are you?" I get up to shine the bike light on him.

"Uh-huh. Right down the line of that tire track on my face," he says, and maybe it's the shock but I lose all control and snort with laughter.

"Don't go listening to the rumors," he says. "Guys find snorting girls who run over them with bikes very sexy."

I snort some more.

"Don't worry about me, I'm fine."

I catch my breath and calm down and we look up the hill and assess the situation. Mr. Tough Guy says we have to walk back up, and I know he's right, but I really want to call the police or the firemen to come and get us. "You can't call the police to help you up a hill," he says. I wonder if my dad could drive his taxi down here. If he knew I was with a boy, he probably could.

"Okay, we walk," I say. "But first I'm calling Jazz so someone knows where we are." We leave the bike light on between us and he limps over to a rock and sits down. He's far enough away so he probably can't hear me but I move even farther from him to make sure.

"Are you chewing gum?" I ask when Jazz finally picks up.

"Yeah. Wait a sec."

"Oh," I say, putting the pieces together, thinking back to the chewing noises at the party. It's weird but I feel the tiniest bit jealous.

"Okay, I'm back," she says. "Where are you?"

"At the bottom of a dark hill with a boy."

There's silence for a couple of seconds. "Is that a metaphor?"

"No. I'm really at the bottom of a dark hill. Ed and I rolled down it on my bike."

"Are you okay?"

"A little shaky but fine." I look quickly over my shoulder to check that Ed's still far away on his rock, and then I whisper, "Ed's funny."

"Something's going on, isn't it?" She moves away from the phone for a second, and I hear her yelling across the crowd, "Daisy, Leo, something's going on with Ed and Lucy."

Oh my God.

"Okay, I'm back."

"I can't believe you did that. Leo will tell Ed that I said something's going on. It isn't. He's with Beth," I whisper.

"Really? She's here, you know. Talking to Leo."

"There as in within earshot of you yelling that something's going on with me and her boyfriend?"

"I didn't think about that. Hang on. I'll fix it."

"No, don't!"

But she's gone, and I hear her yelling, "Lucy just wishes

something was going on, but Ed has a girlfriend so there's nothing." She comes back. "All fixed."

"All fixed? Now they think I'm delusional. I have to go." And find a way to split my conscious self from my unconscious self so I can erase this memory.

"Wait," she says. "We haven't talked about Leo. We've danced but there's no action."

"What was that noise when you answered?"

"I told you. I was chewing gum."

"I thought you were kissing and being shy about saying it."

"You were there when I ran into oncoming traffic to get Jacob's phone number, right? I'm not shy, Luce."

True. And she does love gum. "So you've put out the signals?"

"I'm a lighthouse. He's got something else on his mind. We're playing the question game, and he keeps looking at his watch. I say, 'Is there somewhere you have to go?' And he says, 'I need to be somewhere at one. I can come back to the party and get you after that.' And I say, 'I'll go with you.' And he says, 'No, you can't come with me.' And I think, Well, he's not interested.

"But then he picks up one of my plaits and he twirls it, Luce. Maybe he's thinking about Emma. Maybe he's meeting Emma later. It's driving me crazy. Should I ask Daisy to kick Dylan in the balls so I can find out?"

"It might ruin the mood."

"The mood is dead for those two. Dylan's been trying to dance with her but she's dancing with a guy called Gorilla. I think she's mad about something more than the eggs. It's sad to watch. He's sitting in a corner now, staring at the two of them. Hang on. Beth's telling me something."

"Beth?" Oh my God.

"Okay," Jazz says. "I've got news. Beth says she and Ed broke up about three months ago."

I think about that. I think about that some more. "That's bad, bad news."

"How do you figure? If you want him, he's free."

"He's free and he doesn't want me to know he's free because he doesn't want me to think there's even the possibility of us getting together."

"Are you okay? Your whispers have gone kind of high-pitched."

"I'm fine. I don't even like him like that."

"This is me you're talking to."

"Okay. Maybe I like him a little like that. I don't know. I'm confused. I ran over him with my bike on the way down."

"You might want to ease up on the assault and battery if you do like him."

"No. I'm out here looking for Shadow. I should stick to the plan."

"Maybe Ed's playing hard to get," she says. "That's romantic."

"Lying isn't my idea of romance."

"Your idea of romance requires a corset and a time machine. Loosen up for once. Hang on. Leo wants to talk to Ed."

She's gone before I have a chance to tell her the pieces

I've learned about Leo. I walk over to Ed and hand him the phone. He walks to where I was, and I sit on his rock. I try as hard as I can to hear him, but his voice is too low for me to catch more than the occasional word.

Jazz says the universe tells us answers. I always thought that was stupid, but no one else is giving me anything to go on, so it might be time for last resorts.

I take out a coin and flip it. Heads means Ed didn't tell me about Beth because he was playing hard to get. Okay. Best out of three. Best out of four. Okay, best out of five. Oh well, there's always Shadow.

I stare at the coin in my hand for a while and do some tricks like Dad taught me. I fold it around my fingers, making it appear and disappear. "It's about what you make your audience believe," Dad always says. "But it's also about what your audience is willing to believe. People want to see you magically pull a coin from your ear. So if you're quick enough, if you hide things well enough, they'll believe."

Heads it's Ed. Tails it's Shadow. I flip the coin one last time and wait for it to fall.

ED

I watch Lucy talking to Jazz, and think about how I can tell her. Maybe I could do it while we're standing in front of that wall in the skate park. Or take her to the one I did of Bert. Introduce them, sort of.

Or I could show her the scales I drew near the docks. Like those ones I saw in the Vermeer painting, *Woman Holding a Balance*. Mrs. J. told me once that those scales in his painting weighed something important, something like actions or a soul. Bert and me went to the Vermeer exhibition and while we were looking at that painting I asked him, "What do you think someone's got to do to make a soul heavy?"

"I don't know about souls, but a person should live good. No point living if you don't live good."

While she's on the phone, Lucy looks at me every now and then. The only thing I can hear is her occasionally saying, "Oh my God. Don't. No."

Leo, what have you told Jazz? I try to think of ways to

explain why I lied. After a while she walks over and hands me the phone. "Everything okay?" I ask.

"Everything's fine," she says, and smiles, and I breathe easy again. Easy breathing, I think as I walk away from her and turn my back. I hear Leo laughing before I put it to my ear. "You fell over the drop?" he asks. "Hilarious."

"Hilarious," I whisper. "It's dark and we can't call the cops to help us because I'm robbing a place later. I don't want them getting the idea that Lucy has anything to do with it if I get caught."

Leo stops laughing. "Yeah, definitely don't call the cops. Listen, Dylan and me are leaving to pick up the van soon. We're coming back to get Jazz and Daisy, and then we can swing by the park about one-thirty. You'll be at the top by then."

I lower my voice even further. "You can't drive them around in the getaway van."

"How about we don't call it the getaway van? People might get suspicious."

"So what should we call it?"

"How about the van?"

"It doesn't change what it is and that it's a shitty thing to do. Someone might see them in it." I look back at Lucy, who's sitting in a pool of bike light flipping a coin. "I don't want her in this."

"There's something going on, isn't there?"

"There's nothing going on. Don't go telling Jazz there's something going on."

"That's what you said in year five when Mrs. Peri accused us of being up to something but she couldn't work out what it was. She was frothing at the mouth, and you kept saying, 'There's nothing going on.'"

"So?"

"So you had the class fish down your pants. There was something going on."

"Tell Jazz I had a fish down my pants and we're done."

There's a few beats of silence before he says, "What do you think about the Jazz Lady? She has these little plaits. I like those little plaits. She points her finger a lot. She knows some good poetry. I recited a few of mine and she really liked them."

"You recited stuff from the walls?"

"Relax. Not that. Other stuff."

"What other stuff?"

"Stuff. Don't worry about it."

"I'm not worried about it. I just didn't know you wrote poetry other than for our pieces. Would you say you're more a poet or a social commentator?" I ask, thinking about what Lucy said earlier.

"I don't know." He chuckles. "Would you say you're more of an idiot or a wanker?"

"Fair point."

"So what do you think of the Jazz Lady?"

"I think you actually like her, so don't do something that'll wreck it. Walk her home and pick up the getaway van and hope you don't get arrested tonight."

"It's not technically the getaway van till we get away in it. That's two hours from now, give or take. So how about we pick you up near the skate park, go get some food, have a laugh, drop the girls home, and then, you know."

While I'm thinking about it he says, "By the way, Beth's here looking for you. She says she's got some things to say. She tried your mobile. I told her the phone company cut it off because you're broke."

"Thanks."

"She doesn't care about that stuff. She wants to get back with you. Should I bring her in the van?"

"Don't get her involved in this. I'll call her from a pay phone. Listen, Lucy still thinks I'm with Beth, so don't tell Jazz I'm not."

I don't like the dead-man quiet that comes after what I just said. "Leo?"

"Look. Jazz told me that there might be something going on with you and Lucy because Lucy hinted there might be and Beth heard Jazz and so Jazz told her there wasn't anything going on because you two were dating and Beth said you two hadn't dated in about three months."

"Fuck."

"It's not all bad," he says, and I hang up while he's still talking.

I walk over to Lucy. She's spun a coin in the air, so I catch it and put it on the back of my hand. "What are you doing?"

"Asking the universe questions."

"The universe just dumped you over the side of a steep

hill. You really want to ask it questions?" She doesn't laugh. I follow my instinct and cover my nose in case she breaks it again.

"I can't ask you," she says. "You're a liar."

"Okay, elbows in and stay calm."

"It's not funny, mister."

"What do you care if I'm not going out with Beth? You're on an all-night adventure to find Shadow so you can do it with him."

"Lie down," she says. "I want to get my bike and finish the job."

We stand there for a while, and I don't know what to say. "Do you want to know what the universe told you?" I hold up the coin.

"Actually, I don't." She grabs it from me and puts it in her pocket without looking. Then she wraps her bike helmet strap around and around one handlebar and clicks the clasp. I get the feeling she's imagining the bar is my neck. She starts walking and I pick up the bike.

"Just leave it," she yells. "It's too heavy."

"It's not too heavy," I yell back. "It's fine. Leo's meeting us at the skate park with a van. We can throw it in the back."

"Excellent," she says.

"Excellent," I say, and we stumble over rocks under our feet.

Bert's huffing beside us on the walk up the hill. He's telling me I should say sorry. "You're acting like a heel," he said that time Beth came into the shop to bring my things back.

"No one says *heel* anymore," I told him.

"Laugh all you want, but I still got my girl."

I heave the bike higher on my shoulders. It is too heavy but I'll feel better if I have the option of my own getaway ride when we reach the top. Plus, I feel like a heel, and I'm trying to make it up to her.

"Move it along," Lucy says. "I don't want to miss Leo and Jazz."

Seems my efforts aren't working. "Listen, I lied about Beth because of the way you were looking at me earlier. Like I was a bag of nothing about to grab you."

"But then we got friendly and you still didn't tell me."

"You just ran over me on your bike. When exactly did we get friendly?" But we did talk and we did get friendly and I know it and I should have told her. "I'm sorry."

"Is there anything else you lied about?" she asks.

Now's my chance. I'm Shadow. I've lost my job. I can barely read. I'm robbing your school later so I can pay my rent and help Leo clear his debt with Malcolm Dove. "Uh-uh. Nothing. I broke up with my girlfriend and I didn't feel like talking about it and that's it."

Gutless wonder, Bert says.

"Why'd you break up with her?" Lucy asks.

"It doesn't matter now. It's done."

I don't want to talk about Beth stuff with Lucy. I'm already swimming in the swampy part of the river because I kind of like them both, which would be shitty only I don't have a chance with either of them, so who cares? Beth might think she wants to get back with me but she doesn't. She doesn't know all of me.

She told me to read this book she was studying in literature class. "It's about Vermeer," she said. "You like him." So I sat there, every night, reading a page or two. But my head doesn't hold words. They drop out before I'm putting the next ones in. I'm not any stupider than Leo, so if he can hold words, why can't I?

I got him to read it for me and fill me in. I knew all the paintings he was talking about, knew *Girl with a Pearl Earring*, knew the way Vermeer used that box of his to see things differently. Mrs. J. told me about his camera obscura when I was still at school. How Vermeer looked through it and everything was mixed around so he could paint how no one else saw. I liked that idea, so I watched a documentary on him. I knew lots of stuff, I just hadn't read the stupid book.

But I couldn't tell Beth because she was so happy when I pretended I'd read it. We had this big talk and all the while I felt like she was looking at me through that box of Vermeer's. Everything she saw was true but mixed round the wrong way.

"What are you thinking?" Lucy asks.

"I'm thinking I should have had some carbs before we left the party."

"I've got a packet of mints in my pocket," she says, and I get the feeling I'm on the way to being forgiven.

"I'll take it."

We sit on the hill, halfway to the top, and she divides the

packet. "I like to take my time till they disappear," she says, and it's a second before I realize she's talking about the mints.

"Me too."

"Jazz can eat a packet of these in under a minute."

"Her and Leo have something in common, then. He can eat a sausage roll in under thirty seconds."

"You think they'll get together?" she asks.

"Maybe. Leo was asking what I thought about her. I said she seemed nice."

"Nice is too boring. The first week I met her she raced a train to get Jacob Conroy's phone number."

"She beat it?"

"Yep."

"Then she sounds perfect for Leo."

"She broke up with Jacob at the movies and went back the next day to ask out the boy who was working at the Candy Bar on their date."

"Harsh. But not as harsh as breaking a guy's nose."

"You need to let that go."

"As soon as the scars heal," I tell her.

"So after the Candy Bar boy, she dated David Carter, this guy she met at work. She's got a job reading people's fortunes on Saturday mornings at the Kent Street Coffee Shop. He came in and asked who his next girlfriend was going to be. She told him he was going to meet a short, brown-haired psychic with a love of the theater. Three weeks later she told him she'd had a premonition they were going to break up."

"I can't listen to any more of this."

"The last guy she went out with was Peter Copeland. He was Puck in *A Midsummer Night's Dream*. He asked her out before the play, and she dumped him in the closing scene. She said she didn't like the way he looked in tights."

"So how long ago was that?" I ask.

"She hasn't dated since midyear exams," Lucy says. "Her parents are pretty strict about study this year. She's not allowed out on weeknights, and she works most weekends. She's pretty desperate for some excitement."

"You think that's all she wants from Leo?" I ask. "A night of excitement?"

"I can't tell with Jazz. I always think she likes guys more than she really does."

I think about Leo kneeling in front of his Emma wall. "Sounds like Leo's the one who's in trouble."

# POET

DANCE FLOOR

12:30 A.M.

We should play the question game, the Jazz Lady says.
> **If you're psychic, why do you need to ask me questions?**

Because being psychic's not like reading a book.
It's more like watching a French film
without the subtitles.
> **You like French films?**

I like all films.
> **What's your favorite?**

Tough question.
> **You're a tough girl, though, right?**

My top four are *The Philadelphia Story*, *Breakfast at Tiffany's*,
*The Birds*, and *The Goonies*.
> **The Goonies?**

Have you ever watched *The Goonies*?

**No.**

Next you'll be telling me you never read Dr. Seuss.

**I never read Dr. Seuss.**

See, I told you I was psychic. But, seriously, what were your parents thinking?

**(Beer, beer, beer.) I don't know.**

So who's your favorite writer?

**That's a tough question.**

But you're a tough guy, right?

**(I think I like this girl.)**

**My top four are Henry Rollins, Leonard Cohen, Pablo Neruda, and Woody Guthrie.**

Favorite line from a poem?

**there's a bluebird in my heart that**

**wants to get out**

**—Charles Bukowski**

Is there?

**What?**

A bluebird in your heart?

**Yeah, but he's having a beer. What's your favorite line from a film?**

Bond, James Bond. What's yours?

**Where have you been all my life?**

Good line. And I've been trapped, by the way, in a private girls' school.

**(I really, really like this girl.) Do you have a boyfriend?**

I'm working on it. Do you have a girlfriend?

**No. Who was your last boyfriend?**

Peter Copeland.

**The guy who wore tights in the school play?**

Jealous?

**No. (Maybe. Of every guy you ever met.)**

# ED

I finish the last mint and we start walking again. "I could carry the bike for a while," Lucy says. "I have great muscles because of all the glassblowing."

I heave the bike higher on my shoulders. At least carrying it gives me an excuse for breathing heavy, other than walking next to her great muscles. "You say pretty much whatever's in your head, don't you?"

"It's better than saying nothing, which is what you said on our date. I really wanted to talk."

"You made that kind of clear." This time I let her call it a date.

"I had it all worked out. I thought we'd talk about art. About Rothko. Or maybe books. Or the weather. There was a hurricane in the north that day."

She's the strangest girl I've ever met. I didn't know she was this strange when I asked her out in year ten. I'm not sure I would have asked her if I did. "So how did our conversation go? The one you had in your head?"

"I thought I'd say something like, 'Wasn't that Rothko we saw at the gallery cool?'"

"Very casual."

"Well, it sounds less casual now because we just fell over a hill."

"True. So what did I say back?"

"I left room for you in the conversation."

"Considerate."

"So?"

"Okay, so. Yeah. That Rothko we saw at the gallery was cool."

"Do you even remember what Rothko we're talking about?"

"What are you, a lawyer? *No. 301 (Reds and Violet over Red/Red and Blue over Red)*."

She looks impressed. "What was cool about it?"

I think for a bit, remembering how the last wrong answer I gave her won me a broken nose. "For a while, for as long as you're looking at it, that painting is the world and you get to be in it."

I try to put into words what it feels like to look at that painting, but I can't and that's the point. "Art like that doesn't need words. That painting tells you something by pulling you into it and pushing you out, and you know what it's saying without words being spoken." I put the bike down for a second. "Is that what you thought I'd say?"

"No," she says. "But that was good. Better." I pick up the bike, and we keep walking. "If you like art so much, why'd you leave school right in the middle of that Jeffrey Smart assignment we were doing?" she asks. "You acted like you didn't care about any of it."

"Bad timing. Bert offered me the job and Mum needed help with the rent. I wanted to finish the assignment."

"You like his work?"

"Him and Vermeer," I say. "I like them most of all."

"They're so different," she says.

"Maybe. Feels like life's not moving much in either of them. So what were you planning on saying next?" I ask to get her off the subject of school.

"Do you remember the first piece of art that got you hooked?"

"Maybe *io* from *The Spoils*, by Sam Leach. I've been thinking about it lately, since Bert."

"The dead birds side by side?"

"The bird on the left had the best blue on its chest. I thought about that painting while Valerie was at the shop, reading out cards from the funeral. They were all full of bullshit words that didn't get close to Bert's death. But that painting gets close."

The tiny white bodies making shadows and their skinny legs pointing at the air. Those birds were small enough to fit in my hand, but the day before they'd been flying. "I felt like that painting when I found Bert lying in aisle three."

It's quiet after I say that. I'm high tide and trying to keep my head above the water while I'm back in the store looking at Bert, lying faceup, his old drawing hands not moving.

Apart from Mrs. J. and Mum, he was the only person who

believed I was more than some loser painting on the side of his shop. When I made a mistake, he pointed it out and that was it. He never went on about it the way some people did.

"What do you miss the most about him?" Lucy asks.

That's easy. "I miss the look he'd get on his face when he swore and then checked to see if Valerie had heard. I miss going to galleries with him. Sitting in the storeroom, having a beer. Watching him draw."

We're at the top of the hill now and we sit to rest for a while. Before I met Bert, I was pissed off at my dad and I worried that I was like him and I wondered where he was but I never got into the real details of what I wanted him to be. Before I started painting walls, I drew pictures of him. They were always the same as that one in the train yard. Walls with holes.

A week before Bert died, we went to the Rosalie Gascoigne exhibition. Her works are road signs or drink crates cut up and spliced on wood so words and letters are jumbled and jutting into each other. We were standing in front of this one called *Metropolis* when Bert asked, "Is that what you see? When you look at words?"

"Sort of." He knew about the words that wouldn't stick, but I'd never told him how stupid I felt at school and with Beth when she talked about books. I did that day. "I can read that, though," I said, looking at the road signs. "It's about being shoved into spaces."

We walked over to my favorite piece. " '*But Mostly Air*,' " Bert read the title, and we took in the hugeness of the work. A wall of white on wood that went from floor to ceiling. It was almost nothing, but it took over everything at the same time. "Reminds me of my dad," I said.

He didn't hesitate. "Then there's absolutely no family resemblance."

We kept moving around the exhibition and before we left he bought me a book of Gascoigne's works. It was expensive, so I didn't want to take it. "Give it to Valerie or someone."

"I want to give it to you," he answered. "When people are talking about books they've read, you can talk about this one."

Before we said goodbye that day I almost told him he was as good as having a dad, but I didn't. While I was waiting in aisle three for the ambulance to come, I thought about how he probably would have liked to hear it.

"You have a strange look on your face," Lucy says.

"You get even more charming as the night goes on," I tell her. "I was thinking about Rosalie Gascoigne and a book of her work Bert gave me."

"I went to that exhibition. My favorite was *Solitude*. Those black O's and U's on the yellow are exactly what it feels like to be alone."

"It was one of Bert's favorites. That and *Windows*. He liked how she'd used linoleum on the wood and made it look like glass. He said it showed a person had to make their own windows sometimes."

Now that she knows about Beth, it feels like there's not such a big gap between her and me. Instead of two people in the middle of us, there's only one. Shadow. And I'm him, so it's almost just her and me.

"Do you make windows?" I ask her.

She says no. Well. Maybe. Because all glass is transparent, so isn't that technically a window, however small and weirdly shaped? I like how she talks. Her words feel like gaps in the wood, and I see through them to some other place. I want to paint a wall that's like Gascoigne's *But Mostly Air*, only it's light taking over.

"So who's your favorite glass artist?" I ask.

"Dale Chihuly." She pulls out her phone and moves close to show me a picture of his work. "It's an eleven-meter-long chandelier at the Victoria and Albert Museum."

It looks like one of those tangles she drew, only it's hanging from a ceiling. Blue and yellow. A sideways ocean.

"It looks to me like a feeling pulled straight out from under your skin," she says.

"I say again, you're not like other girls." I make the image bigger so I can get a close-up. "Does glass come in that color?" I ask. "Or do you mix it like paint?"

She tells me about adding metal oxides to the glass while it's blown. "Cobalt gives a deep blue," she says. "You can add chromium for a rich green. Gold is a bit tricky, but if you add it right, you get red."

Her words are pictures, and I'm painting them on the wall in my head as she talks.

# LUCY

Ed looks at the Dale Chihuly, and I can tell he loves it too. Al showed it to me first. I was sitting on the steps after my first day in the hot shop, covered in burns and disappointment.

He came out and sat next to me with two books, a first-aid kit, and a packet of M&M's. "That's bound to happen," he said, looking at my arm and handing me some antiseptic and chocolate. "You did well today."

"Did you see what happened when I blew into the pipe? The glass looked like an alien. I can't even blow right."

"When I've taught you what I know, you'll be good enough to make this," he said, and opened one of the books to the page that showed one of Chihuly's chandeliers. "That's what you want, isn't it?"

I looked through all his works, glass spinning yellows and blues and silver. "That's what I want. And to make pieces like your ghost vases."

"You might start off making pieces like his or mine. But

you think differently than anyone I know. You'll end up going your own way. But first you need to study," he said, and handed me the second book, titled *The Properties of Glass*.

"I took it home and read it every night," I tell Ed. "Al put in this quote at the beginning from Lino Tagliapietra, one of the best glass artists in the world. I can't remember it exactly, but it was something like it's not how you make the piece of glass but how you save it from destroying itself."

"How does it do that?" Ed asks. "Destroy itself?"

The problems that are hardest to stop are the ones that are going on below the surface. When I'm making something, I try to imagine it from the beginning to the end. It starts as a basic mixture, of silica and soda and lime, things that are nothing like what it becomes.

But heat them and turn them to liquid and balance the properties and they'll stay liquid long enough for you to change them. Long enough for you to make them almost anything you want them to be.

"All the ingredients in glass," Al told me once, "they work together. But if you don't apply the right conditions, then they turn back into what they were. If you don't anneal it, then the thin pieces and the thick pieces cool at different rates, and that causes tension in your work. Those tensions pull the piece apart."

Chihuly understands glass, so he can change it into ice, into flowers, into chandeliers that look to me like longing and heartbreak and hope.

I don't know how to explain that to Ed; it's something I

know because I've seen it, not because I understand all the science. Al says one day I will know the theory after I study more, but for now, it's enough that I know glass with my hands and with my arms. I can make a piece without wrecking it because I can feel it. And because Al guides me.

So I tell Ed, "If you come into the studio, I can show you. The best way to understand the tensions in glass is to make something and break it."

I remember how Al made me blow a vase and leave it out of the annealer. In less than ten minutes it was ruined. Even so, I took it home and put it on my windowsill. I liked the way the light played with the cracks.

"Can you show me how to make something that doesn't break? Something using cobalt?" he asks.

"I love science," a voice behind us says before I can answer. I turn around. "Hi, Malcolm."

"Shit," Ed says. "*Shit.*"

"Did you tell Ed about Rupert's Drop? If you add a hot piece of glass to some freezing cold water, it always forms a shape with a big head and a thin tail."

"Like a teardrop," I tell Ed. "It's named after Prince Rupert of the Rhine, this guy who was really interested in glass."

"You can smash the head of that teardrop with a hammer, pinch it with pliers, do all sorts of torturous things to it, and it still won't break," Malcolm says.

I've seen it and Al's explained it to me, but I still find it hard to understand. "I think what happens is the outside of the glass cools and becomes solid while the inside is still warm. So that means the inside shrinks, pulling at the outside layer. There's so much stress in the head of the teardrop that it won't break."

"But if you even tap the thin tail, it breaks and releases all that tension and the whole thing explodes," Malcolm says.

"It's very cool," I tell Ed. "You have to break it in water or in a jar with a lid because the glass shatters into powder pieces and snowstorms everywhere."

"It's almost a metaphor for the human condition," Malcolm says. "Humans are strong, but if you hit them at the right point, they destruct."

I think he's being poetic till he pulls out a hammer.

"Shit," Ed says again. *"Shit."*

**ED**

"Shit. *Shit.* You know him?" I ask as Malcolm twirls the hammer around in his hands. "I don't understand how you know him."

"He's the guy I met outside at the party," she says, staring at the hammer.

I look at his suit. "He's the one you thought was Shadow?"

"In my defense, he wasn't holding a hammer back then."

"Lucy and I had a lovely chat about where I might find you tonight," Malcolm says.

"You told him where we were going?" I ask.

"Yes," she says slowly, looking confused. "I thought he was your friend."

I fill her in quickly. "He's a psychopath."

I look at the bike, and Malcolm wags his finger. He's going to break me like Prince Fucking Rupert's Drop. His thugs are standing in the background, shuffling and waiting, shuffling and waiting. They're not people you want to meet in the dark. They're not people you want to meet in the light.

"So," Malcolm says. "Leo owes me money."

"You'll have it tomorrow."

"I want it now."

"You tricked me," Lucy says, clicking it all together beside me. She's gone from confused to angry in less than a minute. I consider putting my hand over her mouth, but there's no time. "You acted as if you liked me just to find out where we'd be tonight."

And even though it's stupid of her to say because we're in what Bert would call a sticky jam, I can't help laughing at the surprised look on her face. Like it's a shock that some guy she just met isn't what she wanted him to be. Like it's a shock that a guy in a sharp suit who talks nice isn't actually nice.

"Don't let him get to you," I tell her. "He eats cockroaches."

"Cockroaches?" she asks. *"Cockroaches?"*

Malcolm grins. "Just the one. Now." He taps the hammer against his leg. "I want you to give Leo a message for me."

"That's it? You want us to pass on a message?" I ask. "Okay." I feel pretty lucky until he and his men move closer and I see that the message is going to be in the form of a bruise on my face. I can't stop looking at Lucy's bike, which is lying on the ground.

"If you try to run," Malcolm says, "I'll give her the message instead."

By now Lucy's out of her cockroach haze, and she's paying attention. She moves close and holds my hand, and I go from scared to mad. Because I've been wanting her to do that all night, and it'd be perfect if we weren't surrounded by a psychopath and his gang of psychets. Because I'm tired of all the crap that seems to be coming my way lately. I want to do something about it, like send my knuckles into Malcolm's face and run, only if I do that he'll hurt her as well as me.

"I'll give you some time to think about who you'd like to take the message," Malcolm says, picking up the bike and walking over to his thugs. He always did love the fucking drama. I remember before he ate that cockroach, he took a second to put a little cracked pepper on it.

"We need a plan," I say quietly. "What we don't want to do is piss him off, so when he comes back, follow my lead."

"Okay," she says, watching as Malcolm comes toward us.

"Who takes the message?" he asks.

I'm about to answer when Lucy says, "Why don't you give it to Leo? Wait, I know, it's because you're scared of him, you cockroach-eating-coward motherfucker."

I look at her. *"Motherfucker?"*

"Motherfucker," she says.

"The next one to call me a motherfucker takes the message," Malcolm says.

*"Motherfucker,"* Lucy and I say together.

Shit. We're arguing about who's going to take the message when Malcolm picks Lucy. He gets closer to her and the world inside me moves fast and the world outside stays deadly still. I feel better for a second when he puts down the hammer but worse when he pulls out a compass and twirls it round his fingers like a naughty circus performer. "I'm going to give her a nipple ring."

"No, you're fucking not," I say. One, I don't want to think about Malcolm if I ever get lucky enough to get lucky with Lucy, and two, I like her body just the way it is. I try to fight but the thugs hold me and I'm all whirl inside, all spin, and as Malcolm tells her to pull up her shirt, I lose it.

I get an arm free and swing at Malcolm but miss and I'm yelling at Lucy to run but she won't and I swing my leg into Malcolm's knee and hope it pisses him off enough to pierce me instead and it does.

He tells me to pull up my shirt and he puts the compass to my skin. I close my eyes and feel the point. It's going to hurt so, so bad. Lucy holds my hand again, which is nice but I'm not really in the mood anymore.

Malcolm stops. "I'll do you a favor. I'll pierce your ear first."

"We need to talk about the definition of a— Fuuuuuuuuck!" I yell as he pushes the compass straight through my earlobe.

That's when it happens. Lucy cracks him in the face. I look away for a second, and then I look back. It's too good to miss. There's blood and screaming and I feel better because I didn't scream when she hit me and I only cried later, which was the effect of the anesthetic.

"That wasn't an accident, mister," she says. And then she goes white and while the thugs are busy checking out Malcolm's nose I pick up the bike, tell her to get on, and I ride, her lightning-bolt helmet bumping against the handlebars.

My legs pump and my heart spins crazy and it feels so good not to have given in to some loser who thinks he can tell us what to do and we'll just do it because he's got us up against a wall and it looks like there's no way we can escape. But we can escape. We do. We spill across the park, spill and fly, and there's light rising from somewhere ahead, from the skate park, from the light that hangs over the wall I want to show her. "How are we doing?" I call.

"I'm about to vomit."

"Well, that's bad, since it'll land on me, but I meant, are we losing them?"

I feel her twist and turn back. "We're doing good. I can't even see them. How is your ear?"

"It has a compass-size hole in it, so, you know. It's sore."

Her hands are on my back and we're rolling through the park, rolling on our getaway bike. The air is moving again, making way for me, making way. I stop at the skate park and we topple onto the grass, close, circled by heat from the air and heat from our breath. "You really cracked him hard."

"I hope he's okay," she says.

"I hope he's hospitalized."

"Do you think we're safe here? He might be chasing us."

"Trust me, I've been where he is. He's not running any-where. And even if he is, by the time they cover the ground we did on the bike, Leo'll be here."

She pulls a tissue from her pocket and it's old and dirty and she'll probably kill me with infection but I don't say that because I don't care. I don't care because I'm close to her now and I see that mark on her neck and I'm back at that wall, painting those lines on a face that's all mystery, all something

I want to understand. Only this time my car's not blowing smoke because she's interested, maybe.

And she looks over my shoulder, touching my ear, taking in my wall. A huge storm, a monster. Waves bigger than buildings. It took me all night to get the blues and the greens moving in and out of each other. To get the yellow sky swirling above the dark waves, swirling above these two figures on the shore. A guy with a surfboard and a little fish next to him. Me and Beth at the beginning. Me and Bert too. Me and Leo.

She looks at it and looks back at my ear, and I don't know if she sees me in the piece or not. How could she not see me in it? That's all I am, some guy on a shore, trapped by waves and looking for a way to swim. "What do you think?" I ask her, but she's back to looking at my ear.

"It's not completely pierced. I think you could let it heal or go all the way."

I'm getting real close, my breath touching hers, and she's not moving back. She's not moving at all. "I choose to go all the way," I tell her, and feel like a complete wanker, but being a wanker doesn't ruin the moment. She leans forward, and I'm about to kiss her. Finally, I'm about to kiss her. I lean in, my mouth close, so close. And then she goes white and I roll out of the way because I'm pretty sure she's about to heave.

# LUCY

Ed's breath wanders over me and it feels like we're hanging from the sky or the ceiling. Swaying around each other without our feet on the ground. If we touched, I wouldn't be surprised to hear chiming. I press that tissue to his ear and my fingers tingle. He asks me what I think, and I tell him he could let it heal or go all the way. He chooses go all the way.

He says it in a voice that makes me think cool, not idiot, and a line like that is one hundred percent risk. I'm not sure of anything, not sure if he means what I think he means, not sure if the adrenaline is playing tricks on me. Not sure if he's the one I like or if the one I like is Shadow. Maybe it's both. It's definitely not Malcolm Dove.

Like I said before, a girl doesn't think clearly when faced with electrocution, and if Ed is a toaster, then I am a girl with a knife. I'm about to say something in reply, maybe ask him what he means or just let him kiss me, which I think is where we're headed, when I have a flash of Malcolm's nose and a flash of him eating a cockroach, and that sour feeling rises in me and I'm pretty sure I'm going to throw up.

I think all the experts agree that throwing up while a guy tries to kiss you is bad. It puts all but the very, very keen off, and I'm not sure that Ed is very, very keen. I try hard to stop thinking about Malcolm's blood, but the harder I try, the more I think.

"It's Malcolm's nose," I say to Ed, so he doesn't get the wrong idea. "And the cockroach." I don't want him to think it's the thought of his kiss that's making me sick.

"Lean forward," he tells me. "And think about something good. What's something good?"

"We can definitely rule out this exact moment."

"Tell me more about glass."

I lean like he says and take a few more breaths. "I show promise, Al tells me. Which is a nice way of saying sometimes I make beautiful things and sometimes I make things that explode."

"You're not an entirely safe girl."

"You're not an entirely safe guy."

"So what's the worst thing that's happened to you at the studio?" he asks.

"I backed into a blowtorch once."

"Fuck."

"That's what I said. But louder. Much louder." I pull up my sleeve and show him the white river of the burn. "Some days I'm in the hot shop and Al and Liz and Jack are moving in this fast rhythm, talking in a language I don't understand

182

because I'm still learning. Sometimes they don't use words at all."

Ed nods.

"Al says that's the way it is. Everyone makes mistakes. It doesn't matter how long they've been working with glass."

The wash of traffic coming from the side road calms me. So does Ed's breathing. I watch him watching the Shadow wall. Staring at the waves and the sky foaming around the guy with the board. "You think it's a tsunami?" I ask.

"Tsunami waves aren't steep like other waves," Ed says. "If you were in a boat in deep water, a tsunami might go underneath and you'd never notice. It's only when they're close to shore that they get big like they are on there."

"I didn't know that. You could be in trouble and have no idea."

I look at it for a while longer. "So he knows he's in trouble, and he thinks that fish is going to save him."

"It's just a wall," Ed says.

"Nothing's just anything," I say. "You paint what's in your head."

"So maybe Jazz is right. Maybe you're chasing a guy who's fucked-up."

"Every single person in the world feels like that sometimes. Like there's a monster wave drowning them from the inside out. You must have felt like that when you left school."

"I had Bert."

"So you had a fish."

He keeps looking at the wall and I keep looking at him,

thinking back to that feeling of electrocution that he gave me in art class. I think about his book that he never showed anyone.

"I've never seen your artwork," I say. "You always kept it hidden in class. Did you make that T-shirt?"

"Uh-huh," he says.

"Do you make all your T-shirts?"

"Uh-huh," he says.

"So you're good too," I say, and he moves his eyes from the wall to me.

ED

"What?" she asks.

And I don't think because if I do I won't take her there. And I have to take her there. Because we've gone too far like this. I want to kiss her. I want to give her answers. I want to ask her questions. I want to watch her work. And I can't have those things till she knows.

So we move. Toward the part of the park where the lights don't reach. To where I go when Leo's not with me. Over the fence that marks the end of the skate park. Using her light to make us a road. Over the fence to the empty lot.

"Should we be here?" she asks.

"Probably not," I tell her. But I keep walking and she keeps walking and I lead her to the caravan at the back of the lot.

No one lives in it anymore, and when I want to paint without worrying who's behind me, I come here. It's light green and was made in the 1950s. I tell Lucy I've seen old photos of my great-grandma standing in front of a caravan just like it, shading her eyes against the glare while the shot was taken.

We walk inside. There's no electricity, so there'd be only the bike light except I keep a flashlight in here. I pretend like I found it by accident and turn it on. We make light roads across each other and at the pictures.

Around the middle of the caravan, I've painted a hallway. And crammed into that hallway are birds. Packed in tight so their wings are pinned against their bodies or buckled at odd angles. Tight so you have to look to make out the feathers and the beaks. Close up, you can see some of them are trying to sing.

Along the hallway are doors like those in my head. Some of them are shut with locks like Lucy's Chihuahua one, and some have combinations like we use at school. Some aren't locked, but they're the ones that lead to rooms with more birds in them.

The ones that are locked lead out to sky. It spreads across the roof of the van, blue shifting into white and back into blue again. Somehow the birds know that the locked doors are the ones that lead somewhere good. Some are trying to key in combinations with their wings and their beaks, and some are trying to peck the locks off.

It took me months to do. Sometimes I'd paint and think about me. Sometimes I'd think about Leo and what life was like for him before he got out of that zoo. Sometimes I'd think about Mum. How she says she wouldn't change a thing about her life. I believe her, but there were nights when I got out of bed and saw her at the kitchen table counting money into tins with labels on them. Labels like "Food" and "Rent" and

"Gas" and "Electricity." There was always a tin that said "Pez and Pens for Ed." It took me a while to work out she didn't have a tin for herself.

Lucy keeps moving the light across the walls and back to me. In the quiet I think maybe I can hear those birds. I wonder if there are real ones somewhere, not far away. Or if the sound is coming from inside me.

"How do you know about this place?" Lucy asks, and I tell her Leo and me know this park pretty well.

"You're lying," she says. "You know him. You *really* know him."

No guts, no glory, Bert would say, so I tell her. "Kind of. A bit."

She doesn't look mad exactly, so I keep going. "I didn't say because I thought you might be disappointed. In him. He's not what you think. He's not a bad guy. Not fucked-up like Jazz said." I try to laugh but it doesn't come out right. "He lost his job a while back, and his mum needs help paying the bills. All that romance you want, that perfect guy you've got in your head. He's not that." I point at the walls. "I'm pretty sure he's this."

She nods but I don't think she gets it, and I have to make her get it now. "He's planning on stealing some stuff later. From your school. From the art wing."

The words are finally out there. I'm painting a wall for us, a Shadow stepping back into the person who cast it and becoming solid. I can't think of the words quick enough to tell her, though, and she's filling in the outline for me.

"Mrs. J.'s wing? He's stealing from other artists? He's stealing at all? He's a criminal."

"You knew that. He's a graffitist."

"That's different from being a thief," she says.

And it is, but I want her to look, really look at this place and see it. See that this is a wall that starts years back and goes for years more. This is what it's like to be me. I want her to say that she gets it, that she gets Shadow and what it's like for him. That even if he's this, she still wants him.

Before we can say anything else, Jazz texts her. "They're in the skate park," Lucy says, and moves toward the door. I sit on the bed and ask her what she thinks of the painting. She takes a long time to answer, but I wait because I need to know.

"It makes me feel sad," she says. "And unsafe. I want to go now."

So I flick off the flashlight and we go. She moves so fast she's almost running.

# LUCY

Ed leads me across the park, and I follow him. He's taking me to another Shadow wall, and I want to see it but for different reasons now. I want to see it because I'm going with him. Strange light and soft steps and insects singing a wing song. There's nothing else I'd draw on the world.

We step over the fence of the park and into a spare lot. I ask him if we should be here, and he says probably not, but we keep walking anyway. I can't tell what the dark shape in the corner is, and he doesn't tell me. I think it's a shed or a tree or a packing crate. I'm close before I see it's a caravan, small and curved.

"My mum has this photo of my great-grandmother standing outside one of these," Ed says. "Everything in the shot is painted, so the colors are a hundred times brighter than they would have been in real life."

His hair is making crazy shapes on the night and I almost tell him but he looks nervous and I think maybe he brought me here to have another go at kissing so I keep quiet in case I ruin the moment.

I step inside, and he finds a flashlight and we move our beams over the inside walls. There's a sink and a small built-in couch and two beds. It looks like the cupboards have been pulled out. Shadow's painted on every part of the wall, and it's the strangest feeling. As though we're in a floating lounge room.

I'm glad I'm not here on my own in these corridors, with the birds that are trying to break into sky. I imagine Shadow working where the air doesn't move and the lights don't work and the windows are cracked to spiderwebs.

"How do you know about this place?" I ask, and Ed tells me that he and Leo know this park pretty well. That could be true, but I get the feeling it's not. "You're lying," I say to check, and I move the light from the birds to his face. I can tell. Ed knows Shadow. Really knows him. They're friends, maybe.

He tells me that Shadow is a thief. A criminal. All the time Ed's talking our shadows are moving and birds are flying somewhere outside and I want to be outside with them, with Ed, away from the corridors. I don't want to be with a guy who'd rob the school.

Jazz texts. "They're in the skate park." I want to go right now, but Ed sits on one of the tiny beds.

"You didn't say what you thought of the painting."

I don't want to talk about this painting, though. I want to get out of here so the rest of the night can happen. I want to know more about the Vermeers that Ed likes, and I want to know more about Bert. I want to talk all night and then not talk at all. I want to go to the studio and introduce him to Al while we eat blowtorched cheese toast. There's too much wanting in me for a dark place like this.

"So?" Ed asks, and I can't help thinking that maybe he wants me to tell him something that makes him believe it's him I want to kiss, not Shadow. I tell him the truth, something to move him out of here. That it makes me feel sad and unsafe, and it does. I hate the thought of someone out here in the dark, painting things like this. "I want to go now," I tell him. I want to leave Shadow behind so it's just you and me.

He flicks off the flashlight and puts it back where he found it. We head back toward the skate park and I make sure my hand is where he can take it. But he doesn't.


The others are in the park waiting for us when we get back, and Ed tells them we went for a walk because I felt sick. "She nearly vomited." It's true but not very sexy.

"You got her drunk?" Jazz asks.

"I didn't get her drunk," Ed says. "I got her attacked by Malcolm Dove. Technically, he attacked me and she broke his nose. We should get out of here in case he comes back."

"I need water before I go anywhere," I say, because I do but I also want to talk to Jazz and Daisy alone.

"Five minutes," Leo says. "Ed's right."

As soon as we're out of hearing range, I start talking. "Okay. You know the part until after we went over the hill."

"Right," Jazz says. "Ed's a no-good liar, and you're stuck in the land of corset romance."

"Right." I take them through everything that happened from there: art and glass, and the near nipple piercing and the cockroaches and Ed trying to save me, and the nose breaking, and the almost kissing, and the vomiting, and the secret criminal life of Shadow.

Jazz opens her mouth, but no sound comes out. Daisy folds her arms across her chest.

"Well?"

"Well, I'd say we've definitely left the land of corseted romance," Jazz says. "Do you think the van Leo picked up has something to do with the money he owes?"

"Maybe it's a getaway van," Daisy says.

"Then I vote we get away in it. Right now. Malcolm sounds completely insane."

I look across at the guys. "They're up to something. Don't you think they're up to something?"

"Could be," Daisy says. "But they're all good guys. Dylan wouldn't take me along tonight if they were doing something bad."

"Sometimes it sounds like you still like him," I say.

"I do still like him, but the idiot forgot my birthday today. *Again*. When he said, 'I've got something for you' this afternoon, I thought he'd remembered this year. Then he threw a carton of eggs at my head."

"Happy birthday," Jazz and I say.

"No," she says. "It's really not."

Jazz hands us both a lollipop. "So the question is, do we get in the van with them? If we don't get in, we're stuck in the park and I never get to know Leo. I really like Leo. We danced tonight and played the question game. He told me he has a bluebird on the inside of him."

"Don't you like tough guys?" I ask.

"His bluebird is drinking beer," she says.

"My bluebird is sitting next to another bluebird who forgot its birthday," Daisy says.

"My bluebird would like to be kissed," I say.

"My bluebird has questions," Jazz says. "So, do we take a chance?"

Daisy and I nod. We look across at the guys and watch their outlines move.

# ED

The girls walk Lucy to the tap and I get straight to the point. "Malcolm's piercing my nipple if you don't get him the money."

"I don't like the word *nipple*," Leo says.

"Me neither," I tell him. "I like it even less when it's in the same sentence as *compass* and *Ed* or *Lucy*."

"Stick with me. You'll be fine."

"I'll have to stick with you for the rest of my life if you don't get him the money. Lucy will too. He's got some dangerous-looking guys with him, Leo. You need to call Jake and organize backup."

"He'll be fine once he gets paid."

I think about the blood coming from his nose and the screaming. "I don't know about that, but at least get Jake to advance the money so you can give it to him now."

"I don't want Jake knowing I owe Malcolm."

Leo looks cagey. Apart from tonight, Leo never looks

cagey. "Why'd you need five hundred dollars in the first place?" I ask.

"None of your business."

I point at my piercing. "This makes it my business."

Dylan looks closely at my ear. "Did he sterilize the compass? Because if he didn't, that'll get infected."

"You know, he didn't seem all that concerned with my welfare."

"And since he might still be in the park somewhere, I think we should go," Leo says. "Lucky we've got a getaway van. It's legit to call it the getaway van now because we're using it to get away from Malcolm."

"I get it, Leo." I also get the feeling he's changing the subject, which makes me more curious about the five hundred dollars, so I ask him again.

"I told you, I needed it for Gran."

"Blue rinses gone up in price?" Dylan asks.

"My gran could take you in a fight, so shut up." Since it's true, Dylan does what he's told. Leo turns to me. "Beth told me to tell you to meet her at the place at five this morning. She wanted to meet earlier. I said you were busy."

"Great. She thinks I'm either with a girl or robbing a place."

"You are with a girl and robbing a place." He pulls out his keys and swings them around. "So I was thinking. It's only one-thirty. We've got an hour or so to kill before we take the girls home. What's the name of the hocus-pocus lady your mum went to see at the casino? The Jazz Lady loves psychic phenomena."

"We've got secrets coming out our arses and you want to take them to a clairvoyant?"

"Speak for yourself. There aren't any secrets coming out of my arse."

"Only shit," I tell him, and Dylan steps back a little.

"Okay," Leo says, "what's your problem?"

My problem is Lucy nearly got attacked for him and I did get attacked, and he still won't tell me why he needed the five hundred dollars. But I've been in trouble plenty of times, and Leo's helped me without making a big deal about it.

"My ear hurts, for one. And even if I wanted to go see Maria, I don't have money for a ticket."

He pulls out fifty bucks. "Here. Jake gave me some money for petrol."

I don't take it because if I do I've taken money from the job and that means there's no way out and I'm hoping that there is. I imagine a piece I could do, a tree with money dripping off the leaves and a guy picking it up. I put a girl next to him and she looks a lot like Lucy and the guy looks a lot like me and when they kiss the money falls softly on their shoulders.

Leo tucks the fifty into my pocket. "Stop worrying. You don't even believe in psychics. We make a quick stop at the casino. Far away from Malcolm. We get something to eat there. We drop the girls home."

"Who's going home?" Jazz asks, walking over with Daisy and Lucy.

"Ed thought he might need a hoodie," he tells her.

"It's over eighty-six degrees."

"I told him he was worrying about nothing."

She points a finger. "Out with it. You're up to something."

"Relax," Leo says. "We're not up to anything."

Jazz points two fingers at us now. One from each hand. "If Daisy has to kick someone to find out what's going on, then she will."

Daisy taps her foot and I stand in front of Dylan. I've seen her in action and one kick sends the truth spilling from his mouth.

"We were planning a surprise," Leo says. "Ed's mum is seeing this all-night psychic at the casino and we thought we'd take you." He looks at me. There's no way out now.

"Maria Contessa," I tell them.

"Maria Contessa? She's the best in the business. The cops use her to solve crimes. My mum's seen her. She comes to Australia like once every five years. . . ."

Jazz keeps talking about the great Maria and I know we're going with all our secrets to see the clairvoyant who works with the cops.

Leo grins. "To the getaway van." He walks ahead toward the road with his arm slung around Jazz's shoulders.

"So you're really not up to anything?" she asks him.

"I'm up to nothing."

"Promise that you're not up to anything," she says.

"Are you and Leo and Dylan up to anything?" Lucy asks while I'm waiting for Leo to answer.

I think back to the night Leo talked to me in the dark,

telling me he didn't like sleeping because that's when he dreamt. Telling me because in the night it felt like we weren't awake, weren't even real.

"I promise," Leo says to Jazz.

"You can tell me," Lucy says, and we walk closer to the road where the cars wash sunlight across the night. I'm about to say it, say it's me you've been chasing. I'm the guy with the monster waves inside him. I'm the guy living in that hallway, the sad guy who makes you feel scared. Do you still want to do it with me now? But before the words are out Leo starts the van and I get distracted.

He's grinning and revving the engine as I walk over. "Tell me this isn't the getaway van," I say quietly, leaning into the driver's window.

"Don't worry. It's better than it looks."

I stop worrying about the rest of them hearing. "It looks pink. It looks like a pink VW van with *Free Love* written on the side in huge letters."

"So?"

"So people are going to notice us." Police are going to notice us.

"People are noticing us now," he says, looking at the girls. "Get in quietly, and we'll talk about it later."

It's Jake and the Jag all over again. Only this time Leo and Dylan and me are the ones being caught, and we're not getting off easy. It'll be the cops dragging us by the ear and not his gran. And maybe Lucy and Jazz and Daisy are getting dragged too. "Get in," he mouths through the window. I walk the way Lucy's gone. "It's got pink carpet on the walls," she says. "And there aren't any seats in the back."

"You sit on the floor," Daisy says. "And hold on to the sides like this." She shows her. "See?"

Lucy nods, gets in, and holds on tight to the pink fur of the free-love van. Dylan and Daisy are on the same side as her, so I heave the bike in opposite them. I stay outside, thinking things through. If I was a good guy, I wouldn't take her for this ride. Don't take her for this ride, Bert would say. If she gets arrested, then there go her chances at college. There go her chances at studying glass.

"Ed?" she asks. Go home now, I think. Go home and forget about me and Shadow. Go home and sit in front of the TV and get up in the morning and make glassed-in memories and go to college. But then she smiles and I think about sitting next to her, so I cram in and close the door.

"Whose is this anyway?" she asks, running her hands along the fluffy pink walls.

"Crazy Dave's," Dylan says before he thinks about it.

"You took the girls to Crazy Dave's?" I ask.

"We waited on the corner," Jazz says. "Leo decided we could go with him as long as we didn't go into the house."

At least Leo's acting like he's got half a brain. Wait a minute. "This van *belongs* to Crazy Dave?" I try to be calm but the calm's not coming.

"Who is Crazy Dave?" Jazz asks.

"Some guy," Leo says. "Nobody. A friend of my brother's." He looks back at me in the mirror, eyes telling me to shut up.

"They just call him crazy because he ate five cockroaches once," I say, and Lucy covers my mouth and tells me to shut up about the cockroaches while everyone else laughs and talks about urban legends.

Leo swings around a corner and we bounce and her leg touches mine. I lean my head back and my ear throbs and the lights through the front windshield flicker and everything's messing together and I want to get out but we're on the freeway and there's no escape till Leo takes the exit and maybe there's no escape even then.

I close my eyes and spray a piece in my head, a wall with a shadow guy on it and a shadowy road in front of him. I feel Lucy next to me, and I want to tell her right now, tell her everything. But those shadows are laughing and asking me, What good would that do? What are you thinking? You can't go back to the bottom of that hill and stay with her there. You got to climb to the top sooner or later.

I had a chance while Bert was alive. I had a place to go every day. I had someone who kept the shadows from my blood. But now there's just me, wandering round the galleries and trying to write job applications full of spelling mistakes. Job applications for things I don't want to do anyway.

Daisy tells Dylan to get lost and I open my eyes to see him aim a pillow at her head but miss and hit Lucy. "Oops," Dylan says, and Daisy gets stuck into him and the two go at it and it's clear they've got just enough love left to murder each other.

Lucy's looking at them and every now and then they try to drag her into the fight but she just keeps watching them like a tennis match, back and forth and back and forth.

"You could have hurt her," Daisy says.

"It's a fluffy heart. It's not hurting anyone."

"Like the eggs, right?" she asks.

"That's what this is all about, isn't it? The eggs?"

"Don't say it like I'm being stupid. You threw a carton of them at my head."

"Exactly. A *whole* carton. I used the last of my eggs on you." He crosses his arms. "It was a celebration."

"Can we maybe open a window in here?" Lucy asks. "I'm feeling kind of vansick."

"You're an idiot," Daisy says to Dylan. "I've been dating an idiot."

"Leo," I yell. "Open your window. Quick."

"You don't get to call me an idiot if we're not dating anymore. I've got some self-respect."

"That's a high benchmark you set for yourself. Only your girlfriends get to call you an idiot."

"Why are you so mad at me? We were kissing behind the sheds last week." He turns to Lucy. "Do you know why she's so mad?"

"Why would Lucy know?" Daisy asks. "Why don't you ask me?"

All the while Dylan and Daisy are yelling, Lucy's getting whiter but they don't notice, they just keep going at it. "Will you two shut up? Can't you see she's sick?" I ask.

"Let me out. Get me out," she says.

"Stop the van, Leo," I yell.

Daisy looks at her. "She's about to hurl. Stop the van."

"I'm on a freeway in the fast lane."

"Stop. The. Van," we shout, and Lucy hangs her head and I put my hand on her back and hold her so she doesn't swing. I really like holding her, which feels kind of pathetic considering the situation.

"Hang on, everyone," Leo calls, and the van moves and I grip her tighter. We stop and she gets out and falls on her knees. She doesn't heave. She kneels there, but she doesn't heave.

"Sensitive, isn't she?" Daisy asks.

I pull her hair back and think how I'd like to get closer. You'd have to be a different guy for that to happen, the shadows say. Maybe I could be. Maybe there's a way I could be a different guy from the one who painted the inside of that caravan. What way? the shadows ask, but I don't have an answer yet.

The others go across the road to the petrol station for food. I look around for a place Lucy and me can wait, other than the scene of her near heaving. "I've got an idea," I say, and climb the fence next to the van. I'm level with the roof but I need to be higher. There's no way to get across to it without standing on the very top of the fence and I think screaming while I fall will probably ruin my cool image.

"You'd have to be Superman to get on that way," she says.

"And I'm not?"

She grins and opens the driver's door a little. Then she climbs the fence and uses the open door to step onto the roof.

I follow her. "Some girls let the boys look cool."

"What girls?" she asks.

I don't have an answer.

"I'm not so cool," she says, lying back on the roof. "I keep nearly vomiting."

I lie next to her and try to get a laugh by telling the story about me throwing up my lunch in the car when I was nine. I tell her every humiliating detail down to the bit about the busload of schoolgirls watching. "Scarred me for life."

"And them too, I bet," she says, flicking that band.

I turn my head to look at her. We're close enough to touch but we're not touching. I think back to the things she said in the caravan, and I don't know what happens now, when I tell her I'm Shadow. But I think I don't get to hang out with her anymore.

I should have been straight with her from the start, but it's too late. No wall I can paint can take us back there. And if I only have five minutes left on the roof of the free-love van with her, then I want to spend them talking. Because I'll miss talking to her tomorrow.

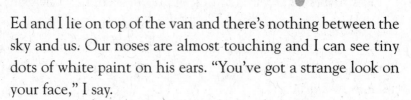

# LUCY

Ed and I lie on top of the van and there's nothing between the sky and us. Our noses are almost touching and I can see tiny dots of white paint on his ears. "You've got a strange look on your face," I say.

"You know, I never get tired of hearing that."

Kiss me, I think. Go on, kiss me. At least grab my arse. It's not very Jane Austen of me, but I'm learning tonight that there's a time and place for Jane Austen.

He doesn't kiss me, though. He starts talking like I wanted him to do on our date. He tells me about the Jeffrey Smart paintings that he loves. He says sometimes he can't stop thinking about those shipping containers or the guy on the side of the road.

"*Cahill Expressway*," I say. "Mrs. J. told me that guy in that painting has a choice. He could go up that hill or into the shadow behind him."

"Maybe that's why I like it," Ed says, blinking. I feel the breath of his lashes.

I tell him the things I wanted to tell Shadow. About that Rothko and how I look at it and see something about love in the reds that bleed into each other. About how Al showed me how to make things the color of dusk and night and love. About how sometimes I wish the world was made of glass. "Then nothing in it would be ordinary."

"I can see why you'd want that," Ed says, and sits up, his eyes escaping with the cars on the freeway. I sit up and watch with him. I'm not sure exactly what's going on. Things between us keep shifting. Maybe it's because Ed thinks I'm still interested in Shadow or because he thinks I feel weird about him lying.

"A lot of people going somewhere," he says. "That blue car. Where do you think it's headed?"

I've played this game before. "To the desert. To red dust and hot stillness."

"The desert's ugly. It's mostly dead, isn't it?" Ed asks.

"Not when you know where to look." I flick that band three times for luck and courage before I say what I'm thinking. "It's okay. That you didn't tell me about Shadow." I flick it again. "I understand why. Things are different now anyway. I think I'm over the whole Shadow thing."

"Two hours ago you wanted to do it with him," he says, and I tell him I didn't know that I'd be doing it during conjugal visits.

"So you don't want to do it with a guy who likes art anymore?"

Let me make this very clear. "Other guys like art. *You* like art."

I move so that my arm is against his arm, and he doesn't

move away. Shadow can rob the school; he can paint oceans. He can do whatever he wants. I'm brushing against Ed.

I scratch at the paint of the van with my nails, and some of it comes off. "You know," I say, "I think this van might have been blue."

"Maybe," he says. "Some other time it was."

# ED

The guys come back across the freeway, and Dylan and Daisy are still arguing. "Why is she so mad at him?" I ask.

"He forgot her birthday."

"That's it? I'll tell him, and he can get her a card."

"I don't think it's that simple."

Nothing is, I think, and we climb off the roof and cram back into the van. Leo takes off and I talk so I can hear her talk back. "Pink is a shitty color."

"It depends," she says. "Last year Mrs. J. took us to this exhibition by an artist named Angela Brennan. It was full of paintings that were so vivid: pink and green and red. I think you would have liked it."

"Not really a pink kind of guy."

"You'd have liked the title. It was called *Everything is what it is & not some other thing.*"

"Be easier if we all called things what they really are."

"What would you do if you weren't at the paint store?" she asks.

"Work at McDonald's, probably."

"No you wouldn't," she says.

No I wouldn't. "I'd study art, I guess. But I don't have year twelve."

"At Monash College, you can do this course that's like year eleven, but if you do well in it, you go through to the university. Al told me about it when I was in year ten."

"So you do all practical stuff?"

"I guess some essays, but mostly practical. Why don't you apply?" she asks.

"No money to do a course."

"You can get grants, and you could keep working at the paint store, part-time."

"Maybe," I say, and catch Leo looking at us in the rearview.


The night's thick and humming when we pull into the casino. It's close to two, but there's still a crowd of people going head-first into the glitter.

We head for the Maria queue, which runs all the way alongside the taxi rank. I guess a lot of people in the city are looking for magic. My mum'd give her last five dollars to that woman for a bit of hope, and when a person's hoping that hard, it's wrong to take their money.

"I got a bad feeling about this," I say to Leo and Dylan after the girls have gone inside to the toilet.

"You've been telling your mum this is stupid for years and now suddenly you believe it?" Leo asks. "Maria Contessa is not going to bust us in front of the girls."

"I can't explain it. But I don't want to go in there."

"I want to go in there," Dylan says. "I want to find out why Daisy's so mad."

"You forgot her birthday," I tell him.

His pupils dilate a bit. "I knew there was something I meant to get with the eggs. Don't go in without me. Tell the girls I'm in the toilet or something." He runs to the doors and disappears into the casino.

"I'm serious, I'm not going in," I say to Leo while we wait. "I'm asking Lucy if she wants to get some food with me before we take her home." I don't want some psychic telling her what I couldn't. I want to spend the rest of the time before I'm arrested talking to her. "I'll meet you back here at two-thirty. Half an hour's heaps of time to drop them off and get to the school."

"I know you're pissed at me," Leo says. "I know why."

"Forget it. I'm worried about getting caught, that's all."

"I didn't know the van was Crazy Dave's. Jake told me to go to Montague Street and by the time I worked out it was his house it was too late to turn back. But I told Jazz she couldn't come in there with me."

"I know."

"I'm not a total idiot. I'm not completely out of control."

"You really like her, huh?"

"She eats a lot of lollies," he says. "More than I eat sausage rolls."

"That's quite a few lollies, then."

"Quite a few." He keeps watching the doors, waiting for her to come back through them. "I wish I hadn't borrowed that money. If I could think of any other way to get it than doing the school over . . ."

"So, we'll think of something. We'll deal with Malcolm some other way."

"There isn't another way," he says. "I've been thinking all night, while she was dancing around me. That's all I could think about. But you shouldn't come with me. It's my problem."

"If you go, I go."

It feels like we watch those doors for hours, waiting for what we want to walk on through. A light goes on and off over our heads, making us nervous shadows. After a while Leo says, "I want to tell her I'm Poet. Not to score her. Just so she knows."

"I told Lucy that Shadow's robbing the school later. So if Jazz knows you're Poet, she'll know that too."

"It doesn't matter."

Leo's right. Maybe Lucy will see that her and me still have something in common. Maybe she won't. But she gets to decide. "How do you want to do it? You want to go with straight honesty?"

"That's the plan," Leo says, and then we see them coming out of the doors. "That's bad."

"Uh-huh." Everything is what it is, I think, watching Raff and Dylan and the girls walk toward us. I just wish it were something else.

# LUCY

The casino's all spin and light. All everything that's inside me. In the toilets we cram into the cubicle of truth. "Ed's the one. It's Ed," I say. "Not Shadow. Ed has great hair. He likes art. He didn't seem to be put off by my vomiting."

"All important qualities to take into account," Jazz says. "But the most important?"

"Static. Definitely static. But he was acting weird on the roof of the van. Something's going on."

"It'll happen. I've got a feeling."

"Do you have a feeling about me?" Daisy asks. "About my static?"

"I do. I think you're going to meet someone who gives better static than Dylan."

"Really?"

"Absolutely," Jazz says. "What you have to do is write a list of all the things you want and then you tell the universe and that's what you get."

"Who is the universe anyway?" Daisy asks. "I mean, people are always talking about it, but the universe must have better things to do than eavesdrop on three girls in a toilet cubicle."

"The trick with the universe theory is not to overthink it," Jazz says.

"Okay." Daisy takes out her lipstick and starts writing a list on the toilet wall.

"So you and Ed," Jazz says. "Leo and me. Everything's turning out even better than I planned."

"I feel kind of stupid that I was chasing Shadow all this time. Do you think I was stupid?"

"That's the way it is. Most people don't know what they want till it's right in front of their face."

"I like Ed being right in front of my face."

"He seems to like being right in front of your face too."

"Do you like Leo being in front of your face? I mean, more than Jacob and the others?"

She thinks about it. "I really do."

"I'm done," Daisy says, staring at her list. "That's the guy I want to meet."

I read through. "That's an interesting list. I never met a guy who'd straighten my hair for me while he's watching football."

"It'd be handy, though," Jazz says. "The back bits are so hard to reach."

"Yep. It'd also be handy to have a guy who makes a great toasted cheese and tomato sandwich." I read further down. "And one who'll work in your parents' fruit store on Saturday without complaining even though he's a little scared of your mum."

"And a guy who still wants you back even when you call him an idiot in a pink van on the freeway would be a catch," Jazz says.

"So would a guy who kisses exactly how you like because you taught him how. These are all important qualities," I tell her.

"They are," Daisy says.

"Daisy!" Dylan calls, and bangs his fist on the toilet door. "I know you're in there! Get out here, I've got a present for you."

Jazz opens the cubicle of truth. "Don't get too excited, but I think that might be the guy of your toilet-wall dreams knocking at the door."

"The universe must be having a slow night," Daisy says.

We walk out, and Dylan hands her a bunch of flowers. "Happy birthday," he says, and she smiles deep violet and kisses him. She doesn't need to know that Ed probably gave him the heads-up.

"Happy birthday," a guy next to Dylan tells Daisy.

"Thanks, Raff," she says after she finishes kissing. "Lucy, Jazz, this is Raff, Pete, and Tim. Guys, this is Lucy and Jazz."

We walk out of the casino, back toward Ed and Leo. Daisy asks Dylan how he remembered. "It came to me." He clicks his fingers. "Just like that."

He's not lying exactly. It probably did come to him just like that after Ed told him.

"So, you two go to school with Daisy?" Raff asks Jazz and me.

"Yep. We've been celebrating the last night of year twelve with Ed and Leo. They're outside," I tell him.

"Pete and Tim and me are celebrating too," he says.

"What school do you go to?" Jazz asks, and I know she's planning on pumping these guys for information about Leo. She reads my thoughts and smiles.

"Delaware High," Raff says.

"So how do you know Dylan?" Jazz asks.

"Him, Leo, and Ed are on our football team."

Leo and Ed are staring at us from the queue. They're standing under a blinking sign that's lighting them up one second and making them hard to see the next. It's the blinking that does it. It's Ed's face in light and shade. It's the way he looks at me, nervous and sad, shoulders swimming downward like that disappointed sea. The way he's haloed with blue from that light above him. He looks fenced in and lost and flat to the edges. He waves at me, and the light makes a bird of his hand.

"Did you know he's Shadow?" I ask Raff, hoping he'll tell me I'm stupid and Ed can go back to being right in front of my face.

"Yeah," he says. "I didn't think anyone except me and Dylan knew. His and Leo's stuff is some of the best around."

The light over Ed and Leo blinks on and off.

Jazz stares ahead too. "Quick question. Are we the stupidest girls in the world?"

"Possibly," I say, close enough now to see the worry on Ed's face.

# ED

I see the moment when Raff tells them. Lucy's foot stops for half a second, and then she puts it down and keeps walking. She doesn't take her eyes off me.

"Shadow," she says when she's close enough to touch.

I don't bother lying.

Leo shuffles away. Shuffle, shuffle. "Don't move, Poet," Jazz says. He gives a smile like he gave his gran that day she caught him pissing on the roses.

Daisy's slower at catching up than Lucy and Jazz, but she gets it now.

"Liar," she says, and drops the flowers on the ground.

I stare at Lucy. She stares back. "All those things I told you about Shadow," she says. "You must have thought they were pretty funny."

"I didn't think they were funny," I say, and move toward her.

"You laughed, though. Quite a lot. So you must have thought some of the things I said were funny."

"It wasn't Ed's idea," Leo tells her. "It was me who thought it'd be a laugh."

Jazz thinks about that for a while. "You thought lying to us all night would be funny?" She thinks some more. "All that time we were talking about poetry and you were quoting lines to me, you thought it was funny? All that time we were dancing, you were really laughing at me?"

Leo looks like he did that night at Emma's house. He stares at Jazz, almost touches her hair, but then pulls his hand back and does something that surprises everyone.

He runs.

He turns around and runs, pushing people out of the way, tumbling through the crowd. All six foot something of him. It seems pretty clear he's not suited to a life of crime. Dylan isn't either, because he looks at Daisy and runs too. Raff and his mates run as well. Jazz and Daisy take off after them all.

I don't run. Lucy doesn't move either. She stands there in front of me. All mouth, all eyes. "I guess we're even now," she says.

"I didn't do it to get you back." Shit, I didn't do it for that. "Maybe at first. Before the party, I don't know. But after." I'm not making a lot of sense, but I keep going because her eyes are pinning me down.

She knows now that I'm him, that I've lost my job. That I'm planning to rob the school later. She knows it all, but she doesn't know why. "In your head, Shadow was this great person, and I'm nothing." Her eyes keep pinning me down. "I can barely even read."

I feel all those years of running and never catching up to

everyone inside me. I'm back on the expressway like that guy in the painting, back on the side of the road with the concrete sweeping round and no way to make people hear or get it because they'd have to be inside my head for that to happen.

Lucy stops looking at me. She stands there not looking and not saying, and I think about that art essay and wanking clowns and that loser of a teacher, Fennel, and those birds on my walls, flapping on the bricks. I think of that ghost in a jar. I think about the hope Bert gave me, which ended with him lying faceup in aisle three, his hands clawed like a bird, old face sinking and old heart not ticking. I think about Leo and the dreams he's too scared to have. And I think how much I want Lucy to tell me something that changes what I think about myself. I want to paint a wall right now and put those words in her mouth, but I don't know what those words would be.

Leo pulls the van into the taxi rank and yells, "If you're coming, get in. It's time. It's *way* past time."

"Aren't you going to say something?" I ask her, but she's a blank wall. Leo's beeping and yelling, but I can't leave till she says something. "Does it matter?"

She opens her mouth and Leo beeps the horn and if she says what I want her to say then I won't get in the van.

"It matters," she says.

And all the birds on that wall fall off the sky. I see them dropping and lying belly-up. A snow of them covering the ground. Later I'll paint that empty sky and the birds below. I'll paint it and know that what's worse than being trapped in a jar is not being anywhere at all.

# LUCY

"Shadow," I say, and I know from his face that he is. I look at him, and the whole night clicks together. The paint on his hands and his clothes and his boots. How he knew where to find the walls. The looks between Leo and Dylan and him. Me saying I'd do it with Shadow and him laughing. Me saying I'd do it with Shadow and him laughing. That last one goes on replay and won't stop.

"All those things I told you about Shadow. You must have thought they were pretty funny." He tells me he didn't think that, but I remember him laughing at me, at all my ideas about love and romance.

He keeps staring, and I try to see him as Shadow, the guy painting in the night. I see him on his own in the dark with all the things he's thinking appearing around him: painted birds and painted doorways and corridors and monster waves. A ghost trapped in a jar.

Jazz is clicking everything together too. She's been talking to Poet all night. Her real guy was fictional. My fictional guy was real.

I knew Dylan was hiding something, right from the start, but I didn't really want to know. I wanted to find Shadow. I wanted flowers hanging from the roof. I wanted to *do it* with Shadow. Oh my God, when I have time, I need to put that in a memory bottle and smash it with the biggest hammer I can find.

Jazz yells at Leo, and from the way she looks at him, I know he's really not like Jacob or the other guys she's dated. He's that horse tumbling through her. Leo doesn't even stay to explain. He *runs*. Dylan runs too. He forgets Daisy's birthday, throws eggs at her, and lies to have a laugh. Jazz and Daisy run after them.

"I guess we're even now," I say to Ed when we're alone. His words stumble from his mouth but they don't make sense and I'm not sure if it's him or if I'm not hearing right because all the conversations we've had over the past five hours are replaying in my head.

I stare at him, trying to see him for who he is, not all the bits that have been scattered tonight. He won't fit, though. Shadow, Ed, robbing the school, with Beth, not with Beth, employed, unemployed. I don't know the truth of him.

"I can barely even read," he says, and then I do know the truth. Then he clicks together, and I see him. His face is kind of lopsided for a second, like he's trying to keep himself together, keep himself in the shape that he shows to the world, but he can't do it anymore and everything in him is sliding out. I look away because it's easier to look at the lights than at him.

Leo pulls the van into the taxi rank. "If you're coming, get in. It's time. It's *way* past time."

"Aren't you going to say something?" Ed asks me. "Does it matter?"

I hear everything he's ever painted in his voice. I hear that person on the beach, looking at the waves. I hear hearts rocked by earthquakes and disappointed seas. I see the doors along the corridors in his head. I make myself look at him, because he needs to be looked at. He needs to be seen. I hate that he's been on his own for so long, painting graffiti moons and bricked-in birds and keeping quiet about who he really is. "It matters," I tell him.

His face snowstorms like that Rupert's Drop, and he gets in with Leo and leaves.

"I didn't finish," I shout after the van. "To you! I meant it matters *to you!*" I don't care if you can't read. I don't care about you not having a job. I care about the lying and robbing the school.

The pink van disappears down the street like a reversing sunset. I watch them go and think about all the times Al tried to explain the tensions that hold glass together and pull it apart. I think about the time he showed me the Rupert's Drop. I thought I understood before, but I didn't. All those secrets Ed's been holding in all night. All his life. Keeping them in held him together. But I hit him in the right place this time. One tap and he snowstormed apart.

I sit on a bench outside the casino, drifting my legs back and forth and waiting for Jazz and Daisy. The bridge lights blink out messages. Go to the school. Get Ed. Give him the all-important missing words and stop him robbing the place. Tell him he's too good for that. Too smart. Too talented. Take him back to Al's and show him how glass turns into something different when you heat it right. When you cool it right. That not everything ends like the sharp nothing of a Rupert's Drop.

All the time I'm waiting, the urge to run after him is getting stronger. I wish I had my bike. I'd ride straight there, but it's in the back of the van. I can't stop thinking about how I stood in that caravan, looking at all those birds with their wings buckled back, scrabbling at the locks. About the way Ed looked at me and waited. About how I told him the place made me feel sad and unsafe. About how much I wanted to get out of there.

Where are you, Jazz and Daisy? Please, please, please let me get there on time. Before Ed gets arrested, let me tell him that I don't care if he doesn't have a job. Tell him he's still smart and funny. Tell him that some of my most beautiful glass pieces have cracks running through them and I like them anyway because of the colors.

Come on, Jazz and Daisy. We need to get there on time. Please, please, please let me get there on time.

Finally, after a lot of *pleases*, they walk around the corner.

"We lost them," Daisy says. "They've probably gone to Feast, since it's open all night. How bad do you want revenge?"

"I want a hamburger and chips more," Jazz says. "So I guess not very bad."

"They haven't gone to the café. They've gone to rob the school. Ed told me."

"How is it possible that I saw none of this coming?" Jazz asks. "I'll have to quit my job telling fortunes at the café. I can't keep taking people's money."

"Some things are hard to see," I tell her.

"Everything's hard to see when you've got your eyes closed. I'm sorry I got you into this, Luce. I thought my night of action would be less full of, you know, action."

"I want to go to the school." I look over at the one taxi left in the rank. "Do you have any money? I've only got fifteen dollars."

"I don't know, Luce. If we get caught on school grounds with them—"

"It's goodbye, college; hello, prison," Daisy says. "Dylan doesn't even need money. His parents pay for everything." She thinks for a bit. "Except our holiday." She smiles. "He doesn't want me to date a surfer."

"Luce," Jazz says, "I don't want my diary entry tomorrow to be: *Stayed out all night. Went to prison.* I have this urge to go home and find my parents back from overseas so I can watch TV with them. Sure, I'm upset about Leo, but I'll double up on the Hershey's bars and ice cream and deal with it like a normal person."

"I don't want Ed to get arrested." Any minute that taxi will leave, and if we have to wait for another, we might not make it in time. "You don't have to come with me." Please come with me.

"Why don't I try to call Leo?" Jazz asks.

"I'll try Dylan," Daisy says.

I watch them dialing. Please, please, please.

"Leo's must be switched off or he's not picking up."

"Same," Daisy says.

I walk fast to the taxi so I don't change my mind. I don't want to think about what Mrs. J.'s face will look like if I get arrested on suspicion of robbing the school.

Daisy sits in the front of the taxi and gives directions while I sit in the back with Jazz. I give her a hug for coming with me. "Thanks," she says. "But I'll need that more when they're fingerprinting me. One thing is for certain. My monologue is going to be fantastic."


"Is anyone else nearly wetting their pants?" Jazz asks, staring at the school, which looks haunted in the dark. Daisy and I raise our hands. "Well, then, this isn't the romantic end to the night I was hoping for. I wish it were lighter. What's the time?"

"Two-forty-five," Daisy tells her. "It doesn't get light till at least five. I guess that's why they're robbing the place now."

"They are so stupid," Jazz whispers. "Why do I like a guy who's so stupid?"

"I ask myself every day," Daisy says. "Actually, you know, Dylan's not stupid. He scored higher than me on all his practice exams. He just acts stupid."

"Leo's smart too. He recited his poetry to me tonight. You know some journal accepted his work for publication?"

"No way," Daisy says. "He really is Poet."

"Ed's smart," I say.

"Ed's supersmart," Daisy answers. "He set all the sheddies talking when he left school. We figured he and Leo must have done something bad for him not to come back."

"Okay," Jazz says, straightening her dress. "We have to save them. So remember. Stick together and run if you see the cops."

I'm not a psychic, but that goes without saying.

# POET

The Casino

2:15 A.M.

**Losing her**

Running from my girl
Past the glitter of the casino
Past the line at the ATM
Past the reflection of me in the glass
Looking scared
Past the sign that says Wrong Way Go Back
Past the fireballs tearing at the sky
Back past the glitter
Back past the line at the ATM
Back past the reflection of me in the glass
Still looking scared
Back past the sign that says Wrong Way Go Back
Past the fireballs tearing at the sky
Till I've lost her

ED

I get in the van and Leo hits the road, making Lucy nothing but a dot. A dot I never had a chance with. "Turn your phone off, Dylan." Leo throws his phone at him. "Turn mine off too. We don't want to make any stupid mistakes."

"So we're still going?" I have the urge to leap out of the free-love van and into oncoming traffic.

"You want me to let you out?" Leo asks. He's not mad. It's a simple question. I say the word and he'll stop. Through the front window the world is nothing but a tangled glare bouncing and moving past us.

"You don't want to do this either. You think this is stupid. It *is* stupid."

"I know it's stupid. So is Malcolm Dove coming over to my house and doing something bad to my gran. And then to you and me."

"Sooner or later you have to stop," I tell him. "Deal with the stupid things we've done without doing more stupid things to undo them."

The van slows and I figure Leo's actually listened.

"The engine cut out," he says, pushing his foot on the accelerator as horns go off around us.

"Get out of the intersection," some guy yells from the car behind.

"There's nothing I can do, moron," Leo yells back.

"Maybe it's the gasket," Dylan says.

"I didn't blow the gasket."

"Maybe it's the transmission," Dylan says.

"It's not the transmission."

"Oil?"

"*No.*"

"Leo, that money Jake gave you for petrol. You filled it up before you lent me the fifty, yeah?" Leo's quiet and I can't help laughing. "Criminal mastermind at work. You forgot to put petrol in the getaway van."

"Dylan, slide across and hold the wheel. Me and Ed'll push."

I jump out and lean on the back of the van. "Lucky we're inconspicuous," I say. "We wouldn't want to do anything memorable tonight."

"Just push."

"You know, when they report this on *Crime Stoppers*, half the people in the city are going to remember us."

"Will you push?" he asks.

"I am pushing. We're not going anywhere."

"We are going somewhere. It's taking a while because this thing weighs a ton, that's all."

Cars roll past and people call us bad things. "You still got a good feeling about tonight?" I ask as we turn and try shoving the van with our backs. More cars go past and more people yell at us. "The general consensus seems to be that we're losers," I say.

"Well, we're not. Can you believe no one's offered to help us?"

"It's eighty-six degrees, and the city's going crazy. Would you help two guys push a pink van?"

"Yeah," he says, "I would."

"Yeah, you would," I agree. "You're a good guy, Leo."

"Strange time to tell me, but whatever. Head for that traffic island."

We manage to get the van across to the island, and we lean against the back, catching our breath. "I really messed things up with Lucy."

"Join the club. I really messed things up with Jazz. No more lollies for me. I wanted to say sorry and I was all ready to do it, and then my legs just took off." He moves his hand quick across the air. "Just like that."

"You haven't had a girlfriend since Emma. Maybe you panicked."

"I knocked over a little old lady, and she spilled her coins. It's safe to say I panicked."

"Everyone panics." I think about me breaking up with Beth. Me lying to Lucy. Dad running away from Mum. It's what you do after that counts. "Tell Jazz you're sorry. Explain that your last girlfriend nearly had you arrested."

"I don't think that's the best way to sell myself to her

at this point." I watch as he slides onto the ground and leans his head against the back of the van. "I lied to you as well as Jazz," he says. "I haven't been mowing lawns for the past ten Saturdays. I needed the five hundred dollars for a poetry course. My gran wanted me to take one Saturday mornings."

I don't say anything because I don't know what to say. It surprises me and it doesn't.

"I was writing poetry. I owe Malcolm because I want to write poetry. You got attacked in the park for poetry." It's like once Leo starts saying *poetry*, he can't stop. "Mainly, I work with free verse. I did a haiku last week, though. 'I am in deep trouble / I owe lots and lots of cash / Malcolm will kill me.'"

I can't stop laughing about Leo's haiku about the guy who wants to kill us. Dylan gets out of the van and asks us what's so funny, and I tell him Leo's making up Japanese poetry about Malcolm kicking the crap out of us.

"My teacher said my poems were earthy. Most of the women in my course are Gran's age. I like them." He looks at me. "Stop laughing."

"Why didn't you tell me?" I ask, but I know why. "You didn't want to make me feel like an idiot because you can read and I can't."

"You're so full of it," he says. "You can read, it just takes you longer. I heard what Lucy was saying to you. About that course at Monash."

"I'm not doing it."

"I know you won't do it. If Bert hadn't died, you'd have stayed there with him, bored out of your brain, because it was safe."

"I liked working with Bert."

"You liked Bert," he says.

I'd get mad, only I know he's right and so does he, so there's no point. I take out the sketchbook and flick through it for a while. Bert smiles and waves, like he's agreeing with Leo. "He was a good guy."

"He was a great guy," Leo says. "He would have told you to apply for the course."

We watch the traffic for a while, coming and going; thoughts of Lucy come and go. Thoughts about Leo's course come and go too. "So, why didn't you tell me about the poetry?" I ask.

"Because I was writing haikus on Saturday mornings with little old ladies," he says. "It's different from writing on a train carriage. I felt like a bit of a wanker."

"You're not a wanker."

He shrugs. "I don't care anymore. I like poetry. Anyone who doesn't like that can fuck off."

"And you're big enough to make them fuck off."

"Exactly," he says.

We watch more traffic and listen to people yell more interesting things at us, and then Leo says, "Bert would have told you to go see Beth."

"I told Lucy everything tonight. Unemployed graffiti artist who quit school before he finished year ten. She couldn't wait for me to get into the van. Beth won't be any different."

Leo takes a while to answer. "She knows you lost your job. She knows you're Shadow too. I told her tonight. She doesn't give a shit."

I think about that. I think about her standing there in front of me with the box of my things, waiting for me to say something. She's been waiting for months. I think about her waiting at the tree tonight, about how she'll feel if I don't show. A taxi slows and stops in front of us. "You need a lift?" the driver asks.

"We could still make it to the school," Leo says.

"I'm not doing the job," I tell him.

He waves the cab on.

"You're a smart guy," he says. "You know, Emma dumped me because I'd rappelled out of that window, and she said it was over unless I stopped acting like an idiot. I told her I'd stop acting like an idiot when I felt like it. Emma dumped me because I chose acting like an idiot over her." He shakes his head. "So to get her back, I vandalized the side of her house."

"Technically, I vandalized it and you gave me artistic direction."

He chuckles. "The course made me think a bit, you know. That we're smart enough to get out of here. We're just too stupid to work out a way."

"That course was really worth the five hundred dollars, then."

He chuckles again. "Robbing the school was not one of my brighter ideas."

"You're not going either?"

"Tomorrow we sign up at McDonald's. I'll come clean with Jake and ask for some help in the meantime."

"I'll put in a good word for you," Dylan says. "But right now we have to fill this thing up with petrol and get it back to Crazy Dave. He'll make us eat cockroaches if we don't."

None of us moves. "I can't believe you threw eggs at Daisy on her birthday," I say. "You two have been hanging out since year ten. You've known her since primary school. How do you not remember her birthday?"

"I try not to pay her too much attention. I figure if I do, she'll work out she doesn't want to date me."

"That's the stupidest thing I ever heard," Leo says, and I listen while he gives Dylan his women secrets. "Don't ever throw anything at them. Every now and then, tell her something you're thinking, even if it's about the rain. Write her some poetry. And stop acting like an idiot."

"I can't write poetry."

"I'll give you one of mine," Leo says.

I get this lucky feeling leaning against that broken-down pink free-love van listening to poetry. I got Dylan and Leo as friends. I had Bert. I didn't have a dad, but I have a very cool mum. I try not to think about how I don't have Lucy. At least Beth doesn't hate me. That counts for something.

"I better call Jake and tell him we messed up. See

if he can come down here with petrol." Leo turns on his phone. "Shit." He checks his messages. "He's texted me about fifty times. *Get away from the school. Don't do the job. Malcolm's doing the job. I told him the code. Are you there, idiot?* I think my phone's full," Leo says, and dials Jake's number.

"It's me." Leo listens and winces. "Sorry, Jakey. I'll make it up to you. Really? No, don't put her on. Don't. Gran, hi." He winces again. "I had to pay for the poetry classes somehow. You don't have the money; you're living on the pension. Okay, I should have asked. No, I'm not coming home yet. I'll be home when I'm ready. Okay. I'll be home when you say I'm ready. When is that? Okay, that's fair. I love you too, Gran. Can you tell Jake to come with petrol to the corner of Flinders Street and Swanson? He'll see me. I'm kind of hard to miss."

"Good news?" I ask after he's hung up.

"Not exactly good. Not exactly bad. But your nipples are safe. Turns out Malcolm paid Gran a visit. She caught him sneaking around the house with his gang and hit him in the nose with her stick. The screaming woke Jake and his mates. Malcolm told them I owe five hundred dollars, and Jake told Malcolm about the job as proof that I'd pay him later."

"Are we getting to the good news soon?" I ask.

"Jake drove Gran around to the ATM, and she paid Malcolm five hundred dollars. Jake gave Malcolm the alarm code when she wasn't listening to make sure things were really square between us. My debt is paid in full. Lucky we ran out of petrol, hey?"

"I'm still out rent."

"Yeah, but we've got a bright future at McDonald's, and you never wanted to do the job anyway."

"No, I didn't," I say, and get that lucky feeling again.

"Why didn't you ask your gran for the money in the first place?" Dylan asks.

"Because I didn't know she had five hundred dollars sitting in a savings account. And if I did, I wouldn't have wanted to take it from her."

"You'll pay her back," I say.

He nods. "After Jake brings the petrol, we can stop at Feast and grab food before we return the van."

I wait around. We talk a bit. We yell some things at passing cars till Jake gets there. I don't go to Feast, though. Leo drops me off at Beth's on the way. "You're early," he says.

"I can wait if I have to."

I jump the fence and head to the tree and she's already there. The sun's not up yet but it's coming soon. The world's thinned to silence. I lean against the tree and the birds scatter.

"I want to tell you some things," I say. "I know Leo already told you, but I want you to hear it from me." Anything else is the easy way and I'm tired of that. "I never read the Vermeer book. I know all about him because I went to exhibitions and watched documentaries but I never read about him. I left school because it got hard. I don't have a job. I don't have money. I'm Shadow. And I'm sorry I broke up with you the way I did."

She leans in and whispers that she knows, that she missed me, that she doesn't care if I have money or not. She traces the blue around my hands, traces the bits of sky left there.

LUCY

Daisy, Jazz, and I wait in the bushes near the art wing. "What's the time now?"

"Four o'clock," Daisy says, her eyes closed. "A minute later than the last time you asked me."

"We've been waiting here for over an hour. They're not coming." Jazz stands and stretches her legs.

I look past her and see some shadows get out of a van, walk across the grass, and crawl through a window. "They're here."

We move quietly, and I get a tingle that I'm pretty sure comes from the thought of Ed, not the thought of illegal activity. We stand at the open window, and Jazz sticks her head through and whispers, "Get out here, Leo." He doesn't answer. "*Leo*," she says a bit louder. He still doesn't answer. "They must be unplugging things in the computer room. I don't want to go inside the building unless I have to. I'll try calling his phone again."

I keep watch while she dials. "Leo," she whispers. "You answered." She holds the phone out, and we all crowd in and listen.

"Yeah, I answered. I'm sorry I ran before. Sorry I lied too."

"We'll talk about that later. For now, get out of the art wing before the police come."

"I'm not in the art wing," he says. "I'm at the café having a burger."

"If you're there, then who's here?" she asks.

"Jazz," Leo says, "get out of there. We're coming, but you need to run, right now."

"Hello, Lucy," Malcolm says, leaning his arms on the window and looking through at us.

"Run!" I scream.

We move through the school grounds, taking the shortcut around the girls' toilets. I'm running the fastest because I've had experience with Malcolm, and judging from his face, I can't rule out that he might want to kill me.

"Are they behind us?" Jazz yells, and I tell her I don't know; I'm not wasting time looking.

"Go, go!" Daisy yells, and takes the lead. "I think they're behind us." She keeps running and looks back, and there's no time to warn her. She smacks straight into the security guard and falls over. "Okay," she says, shaking her head. "That was unexpected."

The security guard looks at us and we look at him and my future looks dim, and then Jazz says, "Thank God we found you. We were taking a shortcut through the school grounds, and we noticed the light was on in the art wing. We think maybe someone's robbing the school."

It's a performance worthy of a Golden Globe, and he buys it. "Stay here. You might need to give a statement."

As soon as he's out of sight, we run again. I've seen enough of Malcolm Dove to last me the rest of my life. We don't stop moving till we're a couple of streets away from the school. "At least they decided not to do the job," Jazz says, the run still moving through her voice. "Things could have turned out way worse tonight."

"You got your action and adventure." Daisy leans against a fence. "And then some."

"I wouldn't have minded a little more romance." As Jazz says that, a pink spot appears at the end of the street, moving through the night like a dot of sunrise in fast-forward. It's them, I think. It's Ed.

It's Ed, and I'm finally going to have the chance to make things right. To tell him he's smart and if he can't read then there's a reason. And if there isn't a reason, I still don't care. I'm going to tell him that I've never had a better night than this, laughing and talking behind our hands. I'm going to say that I want to hang out with him today and tomorrow and the next day. And on one of those days I want to take him to Al's studio and show him all the things I've made. Show him how glass works, how you can heat it and change it. How you can add color. Show him how, after you're done and it cools, it becomes this beautiful thing that you've made.

"Hey, you feel that?" Jazz asks. "The change is here."

I hold out my arms and let the coolness float across my skin. The lightning never came in the end. Just the breeze. I feel like that Winged Victory of Samothrace sculpture that Mrs. J. showed me. It's marble, held at the Louvre in Paris. A statue of the winged goddess Victory. She lost her head along the way but she still looks triumphant. Half angel, half human, wings spread wide. I turn to Jazz. "I'm going to kiss Ed," I say, and she smiles.

The van pulls up, and Leo and Dylan get out of the front. Leo walks over to Jazz and grins, and in his grin I see what I didn't see at the start. He really likes her. She gives him the serious finger. "I don't date guys with prison records."

I watch him take one of her plaits and twist it slowly. "I will not be going to prison," he says. "I'm thinking about growing up."

I open the back of the van, my zing re-reversing. "It's empty."

"Because we decided not to rob the place," Leo says, still twisting Jazz's plait.

"But where's Ed?"

Leo stops twisting and looks at me. Without him saying anything, I know Ed's with Beth. "Good for him." I sit in the gutter. "Good for him." I lie on the footpath. "Good for him."

Jazz lies next to me on the concrete. "I'm looking at the stars," I say.

"Are you doing that thing where you try to feel small so your problems seem unimportant?"

"Nope. I'm looking at them just because they're not

covered in smog. I want nothing else from them but to be in clear view."

"Are you having a breakdown?"

"Nope. I'm upset. But at least I know the truth about Shadow."

"I'm sorry I pushed you into tonight," Jazz says. "I'm a pushy friend."

"You were right. Real is better. The truth is better. It makes you feel kind of stupid, but it's better." I stretch out on the path. "Chasing Shadow was crazy."

"I like that you're weird. You're the only one of my friends who sees, without a doubt, an Oscar in my future."

"And a Golden Globe," I say. I blow a little statue in the air above us.

"Is she okay?" Leo asks.

"She's fine," Jazz says. "Come and join us on the footpath. We're checking out the stars." We lie side by side and listen to Dylan and Daisy talking in the background.

"I'm sorry I threw eggs at you on your birthday," he says.

"Just write the date somewhere so you don't forget it next year."

"Okay. What was the date yesterday?"

"The nineteenth of October," we all shout.

"So does this mean we'll still be together next year?" he asks.

"It means you can be hopeful," Daisy tells him. "But you can't lie to me again."

"If I can't lie, you can't call me stupid," he says.

"That's fair."

He takes a piece of paper out of his pocket and reads: "'If my like for you was a football crowd, you'd be deaf 'cause of the roar. And if my like for you was a boxer, there'd be a dead guy lying on the floor. And if my like for you was sugar, you'd lose your teeth before you were twenty. And if my like for you was money, let's just say you'd be spending plenty.'"

"You didn't write that, did you?" Daisy asks.

"They're my ideas. Leo made them rhyme."

"Good enough," she says, and puts the paper in her pocket.

I get up after a while and take my bike out of the back of the van. It's a bit banged up but still in working order. I untie my helmet and put it on. I ride down the streets slowly, a cool wind on my skin. The glassy darkness will be gone soon, and the day will be starting up. Birds go crazy, and the world belongs to them for now. And to me. I ride from one side of the road to the other. I'm not thinking of last night as the time I got dumped for Beth. Or the time when I almost kissed Shadow. I'm thinking of it as an adventure. The start of something real.

# POET

## Here

She says she'll forgive me
She says just this one time
She says get on with it and kiss me
She says do that twirling thing with my hair
She says that was exactly what I was after
She says she's glad the cool change has come
I say I'll see her tomorrow
She points a finger at the sky
And says it's here

**ED**

Beth stops whispering in my ear because she knows that something's different. That I've come here to say sorry and to tell her we're really over.

We sit on the grass under our tree and the morning makes new sounds that don't feel right. If I did a wall of us we'd be holding hands in a night with no stars, wearing matching T-shirts that say THE END.

"Lucy?" she asks.

"She doesn't like me. We're not together," I tell her.

"But you want to be together with her. You told her you're Shadow?"

"I did in the end."

"One night and you tell her everything. I should have broken your nose on our first date."

I fucked up. I made Beth wait for two years to hear the truth. I loved her and I slept with her and I broke up with her without telling her why I was doing it. Even though Bert said there was no family resemblance between my dad and me, there was before tonight.

I ask her if I can borrow her brother's bike, and if she'll come with me one more time. And she doesn't tell me to fuck off. She walks inside to leave a note for her parents and then meets me at the front of her house, near the garage door.

We wheel the bikes onto the street, and she hands me her brother's helmet and puts on her pink one. "Some girls would make me wear that as payback." I point at her helmet.

"But I am a very cool girl," she says, and takes off down the street ahead of me.

Very fucking cool, Bert would be saying as I overtake her and ride toward Hoover Street. I laugh thinking about the look he'd have on his face while he was saying it.

We stop at the wall I want to show her. Me with the grass growing from my heart and her with the lawn mower. She rides back so she can look at it from a distance, and then she rides close again, to where I'm standing.

"I thought you'd end up with one of those guys from your school," I tell her. "So I left before it happened."

"Idiot," she says, but I don't take offense. I *was* an idiot. "I've walked past this wall loads of times. I never once thought it was us. I did think that the girl has great hair."

"Did you think anything else?"

"I thought it was amazing," she says, and she puts her foot on the pedal and takes off.

I ride her home to make sure she gets there safely. She tells me she's going to college. "I want to major in literature. I want to study here and overseas. I want to move out and meet exciting people and write a book of my own." She takes a breath and keeps going.

This is the wall I'll paint sometime. Her and me. Like this. The end is still on our T-shirts. But we're riding through a sweet orange sky now, toward the different things we want.

Beth gives me two beers before I leave her house, and she lets me borrow her bike so I can pedal down to the docks and find Bert.

When I get there, I crack open the beers and we have a chat about last night and about places I might be going. You got one more place to go, he says, and I know I do. Lucy might not want to be with me, but I have to finish things off with her. Try, maybe. No guts, no glory.

I stop off at home on the way to get some paint. Mum's sitting at the table, scribbling her bleak numbers. I kiss her on the cheek. "How was Maria?"

"A load of rubbish," she says, smiling. "Where have you been?"

"Out on the town. Celebrating Leo's last night of year twelve." I take a piece of her toast. "You know he's been studying poetry?"

"No. But I'm not surprised. My boys are talented." She messes up my hair.

"So, how are the numbers adding up?"

She looks at her book and runs her pen down the columns. "We can make the rent. The wolf's gone for this month."

I make her a cup of tea and sit across from her. "I'm putting my name down at McDonald's tomorrow. Leo is too. And I thought I'd apply for this art class someone told me about."

She closes her book of bleak numbers, hugs it, and smiles.

"I won't do it if you quit nursing school, though. We both starve and study together."

She nods and drinks her tea. "I can live with that."

The wolf might be with us now, but he won't be with us forever. I think of a wall with wild dogs running and me chasing them in a McDonald's uniform. At least it's not an orange jumpsuit.

# LUCY

Mum and Dad are sitting on deck chairs out in front of the shed when I walk my bike through the gate. They're drinking coffee and talking. "It's six a.m. Are you waiting up for me?"

"We're enjoying the cool change," Mum says. "And congratulating ourselves on a few things. Like having raised a daughter who finished year twelve yesterday."

"Congratulations, Lucy Dervish," Dad says. "You made it."

"I've still got my interview with the organizer of the art course."

"You'll be fine." Mum smiles. "We went down to Al's last night. He called to see if we wanted to look at your folio."

"What'd you think?" I sit on the ground between them.

"I thought it was the most spectacular thing I've ever seen," Mum says. "My daughter the artist."

"You put me in a bottle. How'd you get me in there?" Dad asks.

"I made you collapsible. I put you in and raised you with string and made you stay there with putty."

"You went to a lot of trouble."

"You're important to me, Dad. So, what are the other things you're celebrating?"

"Well, I finished my novel. And your father is almost finished with his new act. I won't give anything away, but he performed it for me last night and it's good. Sad and very funny."

"Humor without sadness is just a pie in the face," Dad says.

"To us," Mum says, and raises her coffee cup.

"You forgot one thing. You forgot to say that you're getting a divorce. It's okay," I tell her when she shakes her head. "I'm almost eighteen now. I can take it."

"We're not getting a divorce, Lucy. I've told you that a million times. I love your father. He loves me."

"He lives in the shed."

"Maybe I'll move into the shed to write my next book," Mum says. "Maybe Dad will live in the house. Or I might go away for a month or two. You're older now, so I think that would be okay. Would that be okay?" she asks.

"Well, yeah." And then I can't keep inside the thing that's busting to get out. "You're weird. That's weird. You're married. You should want to be together all the time."

Mum laughs. "We raised a very conservative daughter. Too much *Pride and Prejudice*."

"That could change," Dad says. "There's still time to get her onto Margaret Atwood."

"Funny. Hilarious. I'm going into the world of adult relationships. I need some solid advice."

"All I can tell you is to have the relationship that's good for you. I need to write. So does your dad." Mum shrugs. "You see how we fight when we don't get time for that. But we love you. You get that, right, Luce?"

"I get that." I don't get a lot of other things, but I always got that. "It's still weird."

"To the Dervish family," Mum says, holding up her coffee again. "Great, and just a little bit weird."

I guess it's like art. What I saw in Mum and Dad was more about me than them. I watch them chatting and laughing. Who says romance is dead? It's not. It's just living in the shed. "What about firing up your camp stove and cooking me some pancakes?"

"Magic," Mum says.

I take my wristband off and give it back to Dad. "For luck with your new act. Although after last night I have serious doubts about the powers of that band."

My phone buzzes while Dad's cooking, and it's Al. *Shadow is here. Right now.* I think about Ed painting a wall, and I hope it's different from the ones scattered around the city. But I know that even if part of it's hopeful because he's back with Beth, there's still a corner that belongs to me. A corner where I'm telling him it matters that he can't read, that he's broke, that he doesn't have a job. I don't want him to paint me like that.

I put on my helmet and grab my bike. "I'll be back soon."

"Where's the fire, Lucy Dervish?" Dad asks.

In me. Under my skin. I figure I've got enough to give a

little to Ed. I take off under a dark sky fading out and turning pink. I owe him some words. *To you.* It's important to you.

I pedal down Rose Drive, where rubbish trucks are collecting bins and clouding the smell of jasmine. Tangled gardens hold up drunken houses along the street. Please let me make it in time. Let me make it to Ed before the night's officially over and he paints that corner of the wall with me in it, telling him he's less than what he is.

The speckled lights of the factory stars are fading. In the background the city rises, gray buildings pointing at the sky. I like this place in the light as well as the dark. I like the crates stacked up on the docks and the old buildings. I like Al's street, all the industry piled together. I like how his glass studio and Shadow's walls take me by surprise in the middle of it all. At the top of the hill I take my hands off the brakes and I let go.

ED

I spray the sky fast. Eyes ahead and behind. Paint sails across the wall, and the things that are in my head sail from can to brick. See this, Lucy. See me and you emptied onto a wall. See us so big that you can't miss us, even if you get here after I've gone.

Lucy's boss sits on his step, watching and texting. Every now and then I turn to check for Lucy and see that he's still there.

I finish and stand back to take it in and I know it's my best wall yet. I hear slurping behind me. The old guy hands me a coffee. "I like your work," he says. "Shadow, right?"

"Right. Actually, it's Ed."

"Al." He puts out his hand, and I shake it. "It's different from your other pieces," he says, pointing at the wall. "It's good."

"I'm trying a new style," I tell him. "I like your stuff too. The ceiling flowers. I thought they were trumpets, but then Lucy set me straight. You've texted her, right?"

He only looks surprised for a second. "A few times." He texts her again. "I expect she'll come speeding over that hill any second. You're working early today."

"I haven't been to sleep yet. I'm not so much working early as working late."

"I always work this early," he says. "Sun coming up is the best time to make glass. No other time has such great colors."

He walks over to the steps and I follow, and we sit there waiting for Lucy. We talk about my work, about when I first started and what I'm planning on doing next.

"I dropped out of school in year ten," I tell him. "But Lucy said there was a course I could maybe do."

"At Monash," he says. "Smart idea." He tells me all about the course, and the more he talks, the more it sounds like it's something I want to do. He reminds me of Bert.

"The thing is," I say after he's finished explaining, "I can't read all that well, so I'd find the writing part hard."

"Maybe you qualify for a scribe. Someone who writes things down. You ever had someone like that?"

"Leo used to write for me, before I left school. I don't have a folio."

Al looks at the wall. "Maybe you do. Lucy takes a good photograph. You and she could borrow my camera. Take some shots of your paintings."

"And that could be a folio?"

"I'm not sure. But there's a woman I know, Karen Josepha. I could ask her."

"Mrs. J."

"Miss J., actually," he says. "She's Lucy's year-twelve art teacher."

"I know her. She's very cool."

"She is very cool," he says.

We look at the hill, waiting for Lucy, who's taking her sweet time, as Bert would say.

"I like Vermeer. Do you like Vermeer?" I ask after a bit.

"I do," Al says. "You go to the exhibition earlier this year?"

"Me and a friend went. My old boss at the paint store. I lost my job, after he died."

"I'm looking for a cleaner. You got references?"

"Uh-huh. I got references."

And just like that he offers me a job. We go inside his studio and he shows me round. I give him Valerie's number. "You could ask Mrs.— I mean, Miss J. too. She'll tell you I'll do a good job."

"I'm sure you will."

I wander around, looking at the glass. *"The Fleet of Memory,"* I say, picking up one of Lucy's bottles. They're the coolest things. It's like the inside of her head's out there on the table. One bottle in the series has a tiny Shadow wall inside. It's the one I did of a blue sky on bricks. "That blue's exactly right," I tell Al.

I leave a message for Lucy with Al and head off. I'm at the end of the street when I see her, that helmet with the lightning bolt on the side flying toward me. I stop and wait for her.

"Hi," she says.

"Hi," I say back. "I met your boss. He offered me a job cleaning his studio." I want her to know straightaway that I'm not the guy I was last night. I don't know who I am, but I'm not that guy.

"That's great, really great," she says, taking off her helmet and hanging it over the handlebars.

"You don't look all that happy. You look like this." I make her face.

"Really? I meant to look happy for you," she says. "Are you sure that's what I look like?"

"Uh-huh."

"Maybe this would be easier if you covered my face."

"Still a romantic, I see."

She covers her own face. "Before you left the casino, I meant to say it's important *to you*. All those things like leaving school and not having a job and not being able to read all that well are important to you, not to me."

I got something inside me now. It's not much, but it's more than I had. "I didn't rob the place."

"I know. I went to save you."

I look at that spot on her neck.

"Do you think I'll be on the run from Malcolm all my life?" she asks.

"Leo's brother took care of it. But I'd stay out of dark parks."

"You shouldn't have lied to me all night," she says. "I feel really dumb now because of all the things I said about Shadow. You should have told me the truth. That bit matters."

"I know." I owe her something for what I did. I think of that Vermeer painting with the scales. You got to weigh something, in the end. Even if it's not very much. "I like you. I didn't want you to think I was stupid, so I lied. I tried to tell you when we stopped at the freeway."

She's quiet for ages.

"Now would be a good time to tell me I'm not stupid," I say.

"Why did you get back with Beth if you like me?" she asks.

"I didn't get back with Beth."

"Really?"

"Okay, take your hand off your face, it's too strange."

She takes it off and smiles and I think of wall after wall after wall. Green mazes wandering and two people wandering through them. Doorways that lead somewhere good. Skies the exact kind of blue I've been looking for.

# LUCY

I listen to Ed with my eyes closed. There's something in his voice that wasn't there before. The truth, maybe. He likes me. Three colliding words. He didn't get back with Beth. "Really?"

"Okay, take your hand off your face, it's too strange."

I do and we smile at each other for a while. Ed's not back with Beth. My parents are in love, but they don't want to live together all the time. Dylan and Daisy fight, but they're staying together, at least until her next birthday. Leo is a poet and he likes Jazz and that's the score.

I know nothing about love. But I know that I want to kiss Ed. I know that I want him to be happy. He's happier than he was; I see that, now that I don't have my hand over my face.

"I went to meet her," he says. "Turns out I went to say goodbye." He smiles again. So do I. "You've got a great smile," he says.

"My dad lives in the shed, but my parents aren't getting divorced."

"Okay."

"I wanted to tell you. In the spirit of being honest."

"Okay," he says, and he's moving closer, and I'm so nervous, so, so nervous.

"You okay there?" he asks.

"I'm okay. Keep going. Keep going."

His mouth dips to that freckle on my neck. He works his way back to my mouth, and my blood is hot glass, caramel and shiny, moving with his breath.

"You're not going to lie to me again," I say, and he says that's the plan. And I say, "You left school because you couldn't read," and he says, that and some girl broke my nose. I say, "Your artwork is my favorite thing about the city."

And he says, "I did a wall for you. Maybe my last one for a while."

"Why the last?"

"I'm thinking about that course you mentioned. Thinking about working on paper."

"Don't guys like you live for the adrenaline?"

"That was always Leo," he says. "So, you want to see it?"

We walk our bikes down the hill to Al's and look at his painting. "Wow."

"Thanks," he answers.

It's the sun. A ball of burning glass taking over the night. He hasn't signed it. But I know who he is. I know who I am. I don't know exactly who we are together, yet. Ed takes out a can and paints a little yellow bird. It's not like that sleeping bird, belly up to the sky.

It's awake.

# ACKNOWLEDGMENTS

Thank you very much, Allison Wortche. My writing is better because you edit with such attention to detail and with such great insight. Thank you, Sue Cohan, for copyediting so carefully. Thank you, Catherine Drayton, for being a fantastic agent and for seeing what you saw in *Graffiti Moon*. Thanks to everyone at InkWell Management, especially Lyndsey Blessing. Thanks to my Australian editors, Claire Craig, Brianne Collins, and Simone Ford. Your careful editing is much appreciated. Thank you, Elizabeth Abbott, Marcus Jobling, Duro Jovicic, Kirsten Matthews, and Karen Murphy, for talking to me about art. Thank you, Bethany Wheeler, for generously donating your time and knowledge about glass. Any errors are mine. Any good stuff is yours. Special thanks to the young adults who shared their stories with me. A big thanks to my nieces and nephews, who let me ask all the questions I want and never tell me to go away. Thanks, Alison Arnold, for plotting in the car; Diana Francavilla, for your scary amount of knowledge about young adult fiction and film; Emma Schwartz, for your writing advice; and Ange Maiden, for always laughing. And lastly, thanks to my brothers; to Cate, Cella, and Ras; and, of course, to my mum and dad.

# *Also by Cath Crowley*

***Charlie Duskin*** is a musician, but she only sings when she's alone, on the moonlit porch or in the back room at Old Gus's Secondhand Record Store. This summer, she's staying with her grandpa in the country, serving burgers to the local kids and missing her mom and grandmother, who have both died. Charlie finds comfort in her music, but she wants more: A friend. A dad who notices her. The chance to show Dave Robbie that she's not entirely unspectacular.

***Rose Butler*** lives next door to Charlie's grandfather and spends her days watching cars pass on the freeway, hanging out with her troublemaker boyfriend, and ignoring Charlie summer after summer. But Rose has just won a scholarship to a science school in the city, where Charlie lives, and suddenly it seems Charlie Duskin just might be her ticket out.

An ALA-YALSA Best Fiction for Young Adults Book
A CCBC Choice
A Bank Street Best Children's Book of the Year

★ "Charlie's voice is unforgettable: every page sings."
—*School Library Journal*, Starred